BOTTLE GROVE

BOTTLE GROVE

A NOVEL

DANIEL HANDLER

BLOOMSBURY PUBLISHING
NEW YORK · LONDON · OXFORD · NEW DELHI · SYDNEY

BLOOMSBURY PUBLISHING
Bloomsbury Publishing Inc.
1385 Broadway, New York, NY 10018, USA

BLOOMSBURY, BLOOMSBURY PUBLISHING, and the Diana logo
are trademarks of Bloomsbury Publishing Plc

First published in the United States 2019

ISBN: HB: 978-1-63286-427-7; eBook: 978-1-63286-428-4

LIBRARY OF CONGRESS CATALOGING-IN-PUBLICATION DATA

Names: Handler, Daniel, author.
Title: Bottle grove : a novel / Daniel Handler.
Description: New York : Bloomsbury Publishing, 2019.
Identifiers: LCCN 2018044230 | ISBN 9781632864277 (hardback) |
ISBN 9781632864284 (ebook)
Subjects: | GSAFD: Adventure fiction.
Classification: LCC PS3558.A4636 B68 2019 | DDC 813/.54—dc23
LC record available at https://lccn.loc.gov/2018044230

2 4 6 8 10 9 7 5 3 1

Typeset by Westchester Publishing Services
Printed and bound in the U.S.A. by Berryville Graphics Inc., Berryville, Virginia

To find out more about our authors and books visit www.bloomsbury.com and
sign up for our newsletters.

Bloomsbury books may be purchased for business or promotional use.
For information on bulk purchases please contact Macmillan Corporate and
Premium Sales Department at specialmarkets@macmillan.com.

IN MEMORY OF DANIEL HYATT, BARMAN EXTRAORDINAIRE

BOTTLE GROVE

Part One

CHAPTER 1

D *EARLY BELOVED*, T H E vicar is practicing his ceremony. His name is Reynard, tall and bent-thin like a
straw in a drink, wearing a borderline-sloppy linen suit, and
a hat for the sun across his ageless face, and is not a vicar. Lil,
the woman in charge, can usually smell this kind of thing on
people, but she is bent over the tray of enchiladas, her elabo-
rate and expensive necklace nearly trailing in the sauce. All
the food for the wedding is Mexican, although the bride and
groom are not Mexican at all, and everything looks delicious.
There is a bowl of pinto beans with a careful spiral of sour
cream in the middle, for instance, and cilantro scattered on
top, in a real pattern. The food isn't what Lil is worried about.

If this is a story about two marriages, then one of them
begins here. The bride is Rachel, who is marrying a man
named Ben Nickels, very kind and not skinny. Rachel Nickels
might not be an ideal new name, a little garbly with the half
rhyme, but her maiden name is worse. The wedding is at
Bottle Grove, a small forest in San Francisco donated by a
wealthy patron for the public good before you were born, back
when people did such things. There are such patches all over

the city, preserved green forever on maps, Wood Hill, Tank Grove, Kite Lake, Stern Forest. This neighborhood is woodsy, and these are the woods, right where an ugly wide avenue meets a sleepier boulevard, at a corner governed by the forbidding but harmless stare of an old Masonic temple. You might miss the snaky sneakaway, a paved road that winds down to an outdoor amphitheater, terrifying at night, where summer concerts go on. Away from that is a field and a small clubhouse where you can get married.

One might think Bottle Grove is named for its shape on the map, or perhaps a nickname that became official over time, as more and more drinkers left glass souvenirs on stumps and boulders. Wrong. There is actually a Bottle family, still hanging on in the city, and in fact Lil is one of them, still using her honorary seat on the board of directors that surveils the grove so she can peep around at all clubhouse functions, ensuring the park's integrity with her nosiness. She is maybe sixty, her hair done very strictly, and her eyes pendulum the reception room and the wide porch. She married into the Bottles, a refugee from another old family out of money, and now the Bottle money is pretty much gone too, buried in real estate too precious to sell. Everything is getting set up.

The only other persons working the wedding are the Mexican caterers, although they are also not, for the most part, Mexican either—nobody much is, it's the wrong neighborhood—and two barmen hired from close by. Their bar is also called Bottle Grove, and is housed about a mile away, on a couple of commercial blocks huddled around the mouth of a streetcar tunnel. The businesses there rise and fall, a hardware store that used to be a bank, coffee that used to be toys, a Japanese restaurant that used to be a Japanese restaurant. This bar, home to numerous schemes both commercial and personal, is slightly too fancy for the area, not quite hip but trying, and also something of a dive. It's one small room with nice tables and no television, kept dark enough that not everyone can be recognized. Behind the bar is a very curated selection of bottles, an old ringy cash register, and a box of cell phones patrons have left behind. The place would be nice if it were a nicer place.

The man who basically runs it, Martin Icke, emerges now from the one of the clubhouse's unisex bathrooms, having noticed there that the toilet paper was almost empty and so found the high cupboard where the spares were kept—this is the kind of person he is now—and stood on tiptoe to get a replacement and fit it in. He is thrifty and clean-shaven, with pale skin, a little veiny as if his blood were making sure to get noticed. He looks a little like a man who has fallen short, and indeed he dropped out of architecture school and was let go, quietly but firmly, from two corporate hotels despite a genuine interest in genuine hospitality. This bar is the thing he's making a run at. The other barman, Stanford Bell, is black and younger—Martin's thirty as of today—and muscly in a white shirt and narrow tie, setting up the special cocktail, made from high-end tequila and some rosewater, steeped in oak barrels. The barrels—there are supposed to be eight of them—are lined up behind the thick wooden bar, each one about the small size of a picnic basket, to be spigoted into glasses for Martin and Stanford to add flourish and fizz. The cocktail is called the Happy Couple, and Ben Nickels, who is definitely happy, has just plugged in the music, which comes, too loud and then OK, from speakers in the rafters. Reynard, in a corner, frowns. The music, customized, is part of a new personalized network, a small piece in a large and very ravenous company perpetrated by a tycoon so famous that the first syllable of his first name is enough to identify him: Vic, or more properly, *the* Vic.

Outside in the afternoon, a scraggly fox is staring from a hiding place. San Francisco is changing, but there are still these wild places, and Bottle Grove is crawling with creatures who get braver when the sun goes down. The fox keeps staring, its eyes empty and sharp, and there is one woman in her late twenties, a substitute Lil was asked to find, and did, when one of the servers woke this morning with a flu, although the substitute looks pretty sickly herself, leaning against the wall between the bathroom doors, taking a quick swig from a bottle of cough syrup she returns to her pocket, her face sweaty and rosy as the caterers unfold the folding tables. If a story of two marriages can have a heroine, she'd be it, although nobody's paying much attention to her now. You wouldn't think she comes from money; she looks genuinely broke. You might think she's a dreamy person, something often thought of attractive people whose eyes seem nowhere near the room, though maybe she's just had too many unkind people in her surroundings, so she takes her eyes elsewhere. Maybe she's scheming up something too. This is pretty much everyone, save a child, being born way across town to much screaming. No one is safe; this is one reason people get married. One-hundred-something guests will arrive in twenty-something minutes.

"Gail," Lil says to the sickly substitute, "find an apron from Andrea in back, and Marvin—"

"Martin," Martin says.

"Martin, then. The couple was specific with no paper napkins. So what are those?"

Martin is behind the bar and looks over at Stanford, who has a fist mid-twist on top of a stack of paper napkins so they would ruffle out in a pretty helix. "What *are* those?" Martin asks him.

Stanford hurries them back in a box. "Nothing, cap'n," he says. "They were for my own personal use."

Martin gives Lil a shrug and offers her a tester Happy Couple. There is mint flecked into shaved ice, there is a little lime. Lil turns it down like it's a bug. "The glasses frost up," Martin says. "People will want napkins."

"People want a lot of things," Lil says, frosty herself.

"The caterers will vanish the tables after dinner," Martin says. "I'm just trying to keep everybody happy."

"That's a dramatic goal," Lil says, disapprovingly. Earlier Martin had thought she was the mother of the bride, what with all her instructions. Now Martin doesn't know what to think. He hasn't done many weddings; in fact the number is zero, actually. It hadn't seemed like it was going to be very hard. "It's not rocket science," is what the owner said a lot at the first bar Martin worked, about everything mostly, though rockets, to Martin, didn't seem that difficult, just big engines and shiny tubes full of proud men, patriotic and broad-shouldered with their stupid helmets and breathing appara-tuses. Maybe nothing, looking at the tiny bright green mint, is difficult, or maybe nothing's easy. Rather than say something to this successful and bratty woman, Martin just nods. He has a list with him, as always, and writes

no paper napkins!

below where he has written

check barrels
sweet vermouth
champagne buckets tables 1, 4, 5
Lil = in charge
no paper napkins
tablecloths to caterer, tables in back closet
show Stan lime star
Gail—long black hair

The substitute is the only caterer whose name Martin has caught, and Lil is glaring at her now. "*Gail,*" she says.

"Yes."

"*Gail.*"

"*Yes.*"

"*Apron.*"

"Wall," the substitute says, tapping a hand on the wall, and continues the tour. "Rafters. Light fixture."

Lil sighs, and Stanford is laughing. "I'm giving you a chance," she says, but the substitute stalks across the room before anyone has a chance to do anything, and takes another swig of the pink syrup. Martin figures something out. He likes her.

"You look bored," he says. "Bored and irritable and fidgety and kind of worried. What's your secret?"

"I don't have any secrets," the substitute says.

"Everybody does."

"Who told you that?"

Martin shakes his head. "It's a secret."

"*Gail.*" Lil's voice is a blare over the tunes. She's in another corner now, where Reynard has slunk, near a window that stares out into some thick brush. Standing next to the brush is a tall woman with the ambitious hair of an old movie, smoking. What Reynard is thinking, what anybody is, is unknowable and nobody's business, Martin decides.

"I need Gail for something," he says to Lil, and gestures, too largely, as if this woman had emerged unsawed from a showy wooden box, he an impresario. The caterers look up, and the groom. In every wedding is the makings of another. Stanford tastes the Happy Couple and smiles. "You see the limes in the thing?" Martin tells him. "Do them like that while I take her out back. There's a barrel missing."

"Right away, cap'n," Stanford says, already raising the knife.

Martin turns to Gail, whose eyes move everyplace on him, like a pat-down at the airport, and then off someplace else. "Nobody calls me Gail," she says.

"OK," Martin says.

"I mean it."

"Look, nobody calls me Gail either. So what do people call—"

"Padgett," she says.

"Padgett. As in . . . ?"

"My middle name, from my mom, her maiden name. As in, Padgett, let's go look for a barrel."

"I'm sure it's in the van."

"Well, this is a short, unsatisfying mystery."

"There are other things, too, in my van."

"Ooh," Padgett says, and raises her eyebrows. Her eyes sink deep, raccoony and insomniesque. They go through a small pair of curtains under an Exit sign gussied down with cobwebs.

"Like mouthwash," Martin says.

"Is that for, what's the drink, Grasshoppers?"

"It's for you," Martin says. "It's all over your breath. It's none of my business, but pour out the vodka."

Padgett looks at him like middle school, guidance counselor, detention. "Vodka?"

"V-O-D," he spells, "ka. It's a basic alcoholic staple and you have some in your pocket, so stop."

"That's cough syrup. I have a cough." She gives a tiny hack but then cuts it out. "What the hell," she says. They're outside now, in back. Beside the bright-painted catering vehicle is a beat-up van, very kidnappy looking, except for bags of ice piled up outside like they're giving the snatched kid one last tailgate party. Padgett pours out the stuff into a gray dusty patch, ashes maybe.

"It's none of my business," Martin says again. "It's just, the breath. You want to sneak something, the tequila drink has rosewater in it, or—"

"Or just knock it off is what you're going to say."

"That's right," Martin says. "I'm a barman who tells people to stop drinking. I hope to become a doctor who's against medicine, and then a nomad who stays home." The lock works, and the van opens up. There is not much there, and none of it is a barrel. An old milk crate guards the left rim, and Martin reaches in and hands her a bottle of mouthwash.

Padgett swigs and looks at the rustling scenery. It is not dark out, but it is darker in the Grove than up on the streets. The clubhouse has a fancy shape, bound to be a spooky shadow, and the porch, where people will smoke and escape the music, is empty but still creaking. She puts her hand in her hair and lets the green sharp mint from the bottle tide over her tongue.

"There was," she says, "*some* cough syrup in it."

"I just don't want to see you fired."

"Oh, I don't care about this job," Padgett says. "I'm just doing it for the money."

Martin grins and, with an eye toward keeping his pants clean, kneels to look under the van with very little hope. "Um, as I see it," he says, and back in the clubhouse they both hear the rise and fall of the vicar's practicing words, pronounced oddly as if he doesn't believe them, or doesn't know what they mean, *more precious than rubies*, before a new song kicks in. "You? Me and Stanford with the limes in there? All that food? We're *all* doing this for the money. Have you been to San Francisco in the past ten years? It's a miracle this place isn't condos, that the clubhouse still sits here affordably on this here real estate. The Vic gets another nickel every time another hit plays, because it's his what's-it the Nickels are using. *Money.* This is the system we have going here."

"I know. I just mean—"

"Even Lil's here for the money."

"Lil?" Padgett says, in disbelief.

"For the board, anyway, which is money. Lil is the lady who—"

"I know who Lil is."

"Then why—"

"You don't know, let me tell you, it's just that I already got paid. They paid me, so I do not as of now really give a fuck."

Martin is standing up, grinning at her like a silly gift. *Doing it for the money*, he thinks, like that's the interesting thing about her. The only people who would say such a thing either had piles of it—trust-funded or, more likely in this town, got in early on some digital contrivance—or were the rarity of genuinely not caring. Martin wants to find out which one, who she is. On the other hand, she might not stick around long enough to give up the answer, not if she's really been paid like she says. What kind of fool, Martin thinks, would give this dame the money first?

"Stop looking at me."

"Sorry." He frowns into the van like it's an old fortune-telling toy. *Try again later.*

"I'm not looking for that. Just because I'm drinking."

"At two."

Padgett smiles at her little wristwatch. "It's almost *four*."

"And you started I'm guessing earlier than right this minute."

She raises the mouthwash and says, "To the nickels," but he doesn't know if she means money or the happy couple. Right, the barrel.

"There were definitely eight barrels in this van," he says, "and definitely seven in the clubhouse."

"Someone need a calculator?"

It's the tall woman, the movie star hairdo, her legs uncertain and clattery like the first time with chopsticks. Her shoes, too, are a little much, and Martin watches her waver. "We're looking for something," he tells her.

"Well, I thought I saw something," the woman says, and her hand wavers too, out past the porch. "It was kind of. Kind of. Kind. Of."

Her voice stops mid-trail, a lazy pioneer. "*Jesus*," Martin says. "Is *everyone* drunk?"

"It wasn't me drunk," the woman says. "It was a real noise. But what is happening here?"

"Somebody rolled out the barrel," Padgett says, and gives the mouthwash to Martin. The woman cranes her neck a little, if it's good she wants some. They all regard each other, in the woods outside the wedding. There is an age that feels like a last chance. All of them know it. They are all exactly the same age—twenty-seven, thirty, thirty-two—and when it isn't worrying them, they worry that they aren't worrying. It is too old, just a little, to be drunk at day. To be at a wedding without having been wed. The world is marrying off and sobering up, Padgett thinks, and here our occupation is that a barrel has gone missing. People our age encircled the globe when no one knew it was a globe, raised nine children in a shack full of grime and death. This city is full of heroes our age, sitting on piles of fortune from old ideas—the taxi, the bed-and-breakfast, the radio—jazzed up in snappy meetings over thoroughbred coffee, but we, now, are lifting a blanket in a van to uncover a space we know has no barrel, to see if there's a barrel in it. Futile and small, the whole everyday situation, vainglorious and screened-in, and the real injustice, if it's injustice, is that Padgett knows where the barrel is.

"And what is this barrel?" the hairdo woman asks, when Martin has explained in one more sentence. "What is in it?"

"Drink," Martin says, which deflates them all. How silly they are, how worthless and lagging. The arrival of the bride makes the division clearer, to the bride most of all. Rachel almost-Nickels peers around the back, grateful she is not any of them.

"Martin, it's you."

"It's me," the barman says cheerily. "Just grabbing the last of everything. This is Padgett, she's helping out today. Padgett, this is Rachel Nickels."

"Not quite yet," Rachel says, with her borrowed watch and a little squealish noise.

"You're taking his name?" Padgett asks.

"*And how*," Rachel says, like a big salesman. "I'm just trying to stay out of the way. I don't know you."

Her eyes have stopped and faded a little on the hairdo woman, who introduces herself; Nina is her name.

"Well, we'll have aqua fresca for earlycomers out in the field in a minute," the bride says, her voice cross-cultural on *fresca*.

Padgett drops her end of the blanket. "I have to get an apron on."

"Is there something you were here for, Rachel?" Martin asks, but the bride is already saying no.

"My hair is done, the flowers look great, my fiancé has stopped fiddling with his music lists. I'm thirty-one and I'm getting married. It's a life-changing experience, so *no*, that's it, that's all I want."

"She did *not*," Padgett says, when Rachel and her dress go inside, "really talk like that, did she?"

Martin tells Padgett she did.

"People shouldn't talk like that at all."

"They're the happy couple," Martin says. "She's actually been very calm and nice for six months, with me."

"I don't care," Padgett says. "You don't wander around saying you're life-changing."

"At the wedding I think it's OK," Nina says.

Padgett kicks the dusty ground like a kid not getting ice cream. You're on your own, she thinks to herself, in this life, lately. "I still say it's wrong," she says, but Martin picks up ice and starts to hustle. Nina gives Padgett a little look of reluctant camaraderie but wanders back off. Padgett listens to the startling crinkle of something in the trees. Bottle Grove has eucalyptus, the leaves long and papery when they fall, and Padgett, believing the noise to be nothing but leaves, stands for a minute alone in the whispery space, sad and prickled from the happiness of others, while she straggles staring at her future, imminent and inevitable and shaped like an apron. She can't believe it.

The fox is staring, lonely in the brush, at the upstairs window where the bride is checking the mirror and thinking about something, something she keeps thinking about throughout the ceremony. It was Jeremy Tyber who did it, in a shiny car, two blocks from Santa Rosa High School. He stopped first for Darla Rochelle, offering her a ride, in exchange, when she hopped in, for sucking him off. She said *what*, and *no*, and *gross*, and *let me out*, and then watched, eyes wide and gossipy, as the car slid farther up the block and Rachel got inside. To Rachel he said nothing untoward and nothing happened, just a quiet ride and a smiley thanks on the way out the door, but in that time Darla told her tale, and Rachel was ruined in high school, nastily and absolutely. Even nice boys grew indecent when they got her alone, and girls were feral at her. It was something she could not shake, something she took with her, like some bullet lodged too near for surgery. The door handle, meaningless then, bland Jeremy Tyber with sunglasses and a creased belt, loomed large in reexamination, but she could never calculate what insult she had caused to him, or Darla Rochelle, that painted such a target on her, and at night, every zap of a dirty thought was alarming evidence that everyone, wrong, was sort of right about her, even her best friend saying finally, "But you did do it, didn't you, Rachel?" in a plastic place in the outdoor mall, such that chocolate frozen yogurt, the smell and the sprinkles, still makes her queasy mad about it, and she frowns under her bridal hat, with feathers.

It is a story she has told several men, crucial, she thought each time, to their learning to know her, although the time you spend learning to know your lover is also, awkwardly given the story, the time you first put your mouth on their genitals, so the story was too often misread as flirty. It was Ben who said, his legs all jumbly with hers in his saggy bed, "Well, that's awful." Well, it is. Well, it was. She is free of it now, is what she is hoping with a ring on her finger next to the other ring surrounded by a ring of trees. Her marriage will be a story, the wedding will, and it is, though the story is not the ceremony, which most, like the bride, dream right through, what with the breeze and the drony vicar and the smell of the upcoming delicious feast. But then it is later, darker, the sky its last gloomy blue at the top of the trees, and there's a new story in the works with five barrels drained of Happy Couples and the music loud. The one tableful of older guests has gone home, and the bride's college gang is crowing the song's chorus while their thirsty husbands lean on the windows and talk about new construction mucking up traffic.

Stanford takes the curtained exit to grab more ice from out back, and a little noise startles him. It is Reynard's tall shadow, and then his sly eyes.

"Good job out there," Stanford says. "How many weddings have you done?"

"Nine," Reynard lies. It is more than that.

"And you're a, what is it? Vicar? I thought they were only in old books."

Reynard steps closer. "We're still around," he says.

"You're responsible for their happiness now, right?" Stanford says. "Is that how it works?"

"I haven't the faintest idea," Reynard says, "how anything works."

"That doesn't sound very clergyman."

"*Indeed*," Reynard says, like a sea captain, a detective, something on TV, and blows a little smoke. There is a cigarette in his hands, and while it is not certain what will happen next, Stanford lets the feeling settle, the bag of ice over his shoulders like a fireman rescue.

"I need to take this back in," Stanford says.

"Sure."

"I'm at work."

Reynard blows a smoke ring like it's another question. The ice crackles a little in the bag and Stanford looks at him again before heaving his way back into the cheery maelstrom of the wedding. The air is roaring with sweat and cumin, and most of the dancers are in the same small circle shouting along with the second verse so loudly they sound like a real crowd. The groom's smile looks so pleased. Stanford walks along the wall to the bar, where Martin nods his thanks. Nina, her hair askew but still glamorous, leans across the bar, fiddling with a sprig of mint, mid-something.

"—how they treat animals is *important*," she is saying, with very bright eyes. "Animals are an important *key* to how *men behave*."

Stanford puts one hand on Martin. "I'm going to gather empties."

"Yes," Martin says, over the music. "Go anywhere but here, I would."

Nina pouts cute, and Stanford grabs four empty beer bottles and two bottles of bubbly, one of which is empty. He makes a quick jaunt-check around the porch, where two women are nuzzling, lovers or drunk or both, and a guitar leans in its case in the corner, bohemia still striving in such an expensive town. Lil is sitting in a large wooden chair, frown and furniture both looking like they were made for her. Stanford asks if he can get her something, and she tells him not to be ridiculous. He circles the building, the beats of the song submerged inside, and tosses everything but the not-empty bottle into a bin. Reynard is so near so quick Stanford almost drops it, and then it's gone from his fist and Reynard is kissing him right under the rain gutters.

"We gotta take a walk," Stanford says. "I don't want to get fired."

"I'm lucky my work is done," Reynard says, and they desert the party together, down the road farther from civilization. Oh, not really. It's a small wood. But a wild patch, away from the bustle, spikes the feeling that anything might go down. It's dark quick, Reynard's linen suit walking with Stanford's shirt like their occupants have vanished into the shadowiness. The bottle moves back and forth. Stanford feels a little prickly and wonders if he is being watched, and when he turns to face Reynard, the vicar's eyes are burning right toward him.

"They say these woods are haunted," Reynard says.

"You for sure are not a religious dude." The bubbles still popping on Stanford's tongue make Reynard's deception seem clever, instead of whatever it actually is. He's young, Stanford reminds himself, strong, and wants to be here on this path. It's been a while, as almost every man feels, since he's been laid.

"It doesn't matter," Reynard says. "The marriage ceremony is never checked up on. Jump through hoops to get married, but nobody investigates if it's true. It's a scheme. It's a scam."

"And what's yours?"

"To get you someplace comfortable for sex," says Reynard in the dark. "You're not afraid, are you?"

"Everybody's afraid when they hear somebody say that," Stanford says, but he isn't.

"The coyote and the mountain climber," Reynard says, "the barber and the peacock, wife, lover and dybbuk, all equally at home in the world."

"OK, you're high."

"I learned that from the Jesuits."

"Do Jesuits and vicars even intersect?"

"They used to keep immigrants here," Reynard says, his hands swinging invisible around the meadow, "and one bride-to-be, bedecked for the occasion, demanded that a fox be roasted and served at the feast. The fox was mate to another fox—"

"That's usually how it works."

"—and the vengeful spirit of the wronged mate flew into the body of the bride and tricked her into hanging herself from a eucalyptus. And they say her spirit still lingers in the purgatory of this amphitheater, the story goes."

They are at the amphitheater now, the darkness opening up like a galaxy around them. "No," Stanford says.

"It's a real story. You can look it up."

"Nobody kept immigrants here. Angel Island, maybe. You are so full of shit. There's no bride spooking around here."

"So why do I tell you this?" Reynard asks, his voice, familiar from the ceremony, like he is reciting again. "Because you still listen, because in times like these to have you listen at all, it's necessary to talk about trees."

This is, it takes Stanford a second to place it, from a poem his last girlfriend, months before he came out, loved. This vicar plucked it from his brain, or maybe his heart. The title is "What Kind of Times Are These," and Reynard drops the bottle and it's gone. They hear it crack, a busy noise but one that sounds like trouble. They were several strides away, but now find and grasp and open their mouths to each other. Reynard reaches down and has Stanford unzipped before he knows it. The vicar's hands are cold, but then warm around him as he thickens. Stanford is not much younger than this guy, probably. He wants to lean back against something but the only thing behind him is the vicar's other hand and open space. In the dark around him, also, it feels like things are happening. "Good," Reynard says, at his mouth.

"I think I heard someone say something," Stanford says.

"That was me."

"No, something else."

"Stop listening. Feel this."

"*Fuck*. That feels good. Why do you do this?"

"Because it feels good."

"No, the vicar thing."

Reynard's mouth leaves him for a minute. Stanford can hear little else besides his own breathing and the unsteady crackle of feet moving on the ground. "Because otherwise nobody invites me to the wedding," he says, opening his shirt. In the dark it looks like something falling, the white fabric fumbling away from his body, and they move in and go at it. It is nighttime. Quick, quick, Stanford thinks, and they walk almost blindly, almost separately, to the clubhouse when they're done. Stanford tucks in everything a few yards before the porch, but who knows the reasoning behind Lil's disapproving glare.

"Where did you go?" Martin asks inside. "People got thirsty suddenly. We could *really* use that last barrel."

"There's beer."

"Look around, Stanford. These are tech guys, some of them. We must offer more splendid things besides splendid beer. These guests are pairing up and marrying off and when they do, hiring the guys from the hip bar will move some of their money into our exhausted wallets."

"OK, OK." Stanford lifts and tilts a barrel like he's cheating at pinball, almost empty. "I'll do a pitcher of margaritas with a little of the rosewater," he says.

"There we go," Martin agrees, "but where were you?"

They have been, not friends, comrades for a while. Nina is still leaning at the bar and she twirls her mint at both of them. "You really want to know?"

Martin lifts a shaker and maracas it, raises his eyebrows.

"I had sex with the vicar."

Martin looks at the woody ceiling and drains the drink, golden yellow, into Nina's glass. "You dog."

Nina laughs and then stops, her eyes panicked over the cocktail. "Reynard?"

"Yeah, the ceremony guy."

"Reynard Mahatma is my husband."

Martin blinks. "*What's* his last name?"

Stanford sees some mistake possible here, what with the vicar not being a vicar, or at least a liar. "He doesn't have a ring on. Are we talking about the same guy?"

"We're *engaged*!" Nina spits. "You *bastard*!"

She has thrown the drink in Stanford's face—he even gets a drop-taste of citrus in his mouth—but it is not clear if this was her intention, as Nina has twirled to face the door and perhaps merely tossed her drink sideways. The *bastard*! is for Reynard, who stands rumpled and blank in the doorway. All this has happened in the gap between songs. The Vic's system allows you, between tunes, to fade-through, segue, or pause, and Ben has spent a few evenings customizing, Rachel tense and patient on the sofa across the room. This is a pause, enough time for the room to move to astonishment. Tech or no, the male guests aren't able-willed enough to be of use, and Nina parts them, tearing toward Reynard in one long scream. Forty drunk people and just about nobody knows who she is. She gets to a folding chair and, *wow!*, brandishes it at

Reynard, straight out front like a lion tamer, as he turns tail and goes right out. "Fucking prick!"

"Guess it's not the first time," Martin says, looking around to catch Padgett's eye. Her sweeping up the glass, next to him, is Martin's thought, but she is nowhere too.

"Goddammit Reynard!"

Nina rages after him—*Mahatma?*—and when the screen door slams shut the broken glass is the only evidence that something in this long-jolly room has been at all amiss. Everyone hears another crash outside, they're pretty sure, but it coordinates with the new song, starting bright, but not so happy as to make things garish. Martin sees Ben pattering over to mute the music and waves at him like the guys on airport runways. "No, no," he says. "Keep. The party. Going."

The words are loud enough that some people laugh and then this shadow has passed, like a train in the countryside, tracks laid for the story the happy couple will tell about the officiating vicar, who'd so charmed them at another wedding, fighting with his wife at theirs. *Fiancée*, Ben or Rachel will take turns correcting each other, but now the car is peeling out and Nina is pounding at the windshield. It's Reynard's car, vintage and gleamy in the small lot by the clubhouse, revving up the road loudly and slowly toward the city, with Nina keeping pace and trying to get in. "Let me in, you bastard *fuck*," she says, and the door falls open, by Reynard or by a weak latch she does not know. She lands on the passenger seat, buckles in and buckles up. "You spoil," she says, "*everything*."

"Nina," Reynard says tiredly. Petulantly. *Ass*—Nina thinks in fury—*holishly*. "Nothing happened, calm down. You need to calm down when you get like this."

"Fuck you. I want, I *wanted*, to marry you if you said you would stop, or even just be fucking *honest*."

"Nina."

"And don't say *nothing happened*, because otherwise it's a fucking science fiction craziness that everyone just happens to make the same thing up wherever we go, you *sneaky fuck*! Oh, these drugs." She starts to lean her head against the window but the road is too rattly. Through the glass and the eucalyptus leaves shimmery in the trees, the moon looks fragile and cowering, like someone could just blow it out. "You said you would quit."

"So did you," Reynard says, quiet.

"But why—"

"Because it feels so good," he says. "What else?"

"*Me*, is what else. Stop this. Don't turn it around. You keep fucking up."

"You're drunk."

"*You're* drunk. Also. Watch the road. Fucking Jesuit schools, is that it? Is that where you learned to sneak off into the dark?"

"They taught me everything is darkness."

"They did not fucking not. You're a clergyman. Watch the road."

"They taught me the darkness tries, but cannot know us, just as we—"

"*Watch the*—there's a dog in the road!" Nina's voice is terrible to hear. A wild shadow springs toward them, larger, and intersects the windshield. "It's a fox!"

Something happens right away, at the crest of the hill of the road, right where the wide avenue is whizzing by big as

life, headlights and horns. Something shattery. What the
doctor will say is, an old-fashioned way of putting it, misad-
venture. The police will say, accident. Driving under the influence. It happened so fast. I saw nothing. A terrible noise. The
two witnesses, high schoolers who truth be told were on the
way into the Grove for sex, rethink the night, and indeed
much is shuffled around. Nina has an ice pack on her head.
She has vomited twice, although that had already been likely
to happen, from drink. And the fox is not dead and neither is
Reynard, although both have had life-changing experiences,
promised at weddings and meetings of addicts, hoping to
change into something else. And so they do. Let us admit, let
us realize, just as there is a space between married and not,
there is a space between beast and person, living and dead,
and the fox and Reynard both vanish at once.

There is blood on the tires and a crumpled hat, men's size
seven, on the seat. The police look deep in the brush. Nina
insists. The high schoolers leave, and end up sprawled over
each other on a grassy hill closer to the zoo. The sex is good.
The sex was always good with Reynard around, Nina thinks
sadly, recalling other exhausted nights, and when the police
amble back to her, they learn about the wedding—"He was
officiating!"—and head downhill and—this is the rest of the
story the Nickels tell—end the party with flashing lights and
interviews. Ben turns the music off, Lil turns the lights on.
People get their coats. The barmen load everything away as
the police give up. A drunk driver fleeing an accident is not
even a story, so frequently does it happen. Past the porch, it
is very dark now. Nobody finds Reynard, or the broken bottle
in the amphitheater.

Still, for most it's been a good night, if strange. Martin gives the keys to Stanford to drive the van, planning to walk to his apartment, not as ratty as you might think, between the forest and the bar, Bottle Grove and Bottle Grove. The solitary late walk is Martin's almost every night, after closing. He heads on up, away from the wedding, knowing it is nothing but raccoons and skunks, maybe a rare fox, skittering around him in the woods. Sometimes the homeless camp here, but not on a night full of sirens. He is not frightened. He even shortcuts before he reaches the last curve, slipping off the paved path to lean his way through the dirt and trees. Martin does not yelp, not even a snort of surprise, when the streetlamps slipstream through the eucalyptus to show him the figure of Padgett, sitting on a log with her feet up and a cup in her hands. She looks like the cover of an album he hasn't thought about in years. He loves it. He should play it when he gets home tonight.

"Hey," she says first.

"Hey. You OK?"

It sounds like one little kid to another after someone's fallen off a bike, and it makes her smile. "Yeah. What are the cops here for?"

"Runaway cater-waitress. It seems she was paid beforehand and did a shitty job and left early. That's federal time, my friend."

She shivers a little, not from cold, and sips from what he sees now is a real porcelain cup, the ones the coffee came in after dinner. "You are so high," he tells her.

"No."

"I know you are."

"Well, yeah, because *you* gave me the cocaine."

There is no arguing this. The three of them, Stanford too, did lines during the ceremony. Martin sits down on the log next to her, which she likes, his doing it without her offer.

"I had to bail," she says. "I had to quit."

"From the moment I walked in and saw you, I knew you were a flight risk."

She gives him a little shove. He inhales her rosy breath, the tequila in her cup.

"That's my drink," he says.

"What?"

"Stop *what*. The Happy Couple."

"Without the fizzy whatever, yeah."

"How did you—"

"I poured myself some before I—"

"And carried one cup of it here to sit on a log for hours? You did fucking not."

"Look," Padgett says. "I'm sure we can find things to agree on."

He reaches to his neck, and for a blurry moment Padgett thinks he's going to strangle himself, but he just loosens his tie. She finishes her cup. The liquor is warm, the rose flavor a little curdly. But the world keeps spinning, the only way she can stand it.

"What happened to you?" he has asked her.

"I told you," she tells him. "I quit. I split. They paid me already."

"But what's your story that you're here like this?"

"Maybe I just hate this goddamn intersection."

"Maybe."

"Yeah well, maybe I do. I had a friend who drove me home."

She expects him to say "What are you talking about?" but he just says, "Home?" Barmen are used to talking to drunks.

"Home. Most nights in high school. You know? When we all, a movie, or just someone's house."

"OK, I get it."

"Nobody did. You probably don't. He was the responsible, driver's license, seat belt, always sober."

"I've met that type."

"Yeah, that was the problem. Because, you won't guess, I wasn't, always. Sober."

"It's too dark for you to see my astonished face."

Padgett's arm rises, as if to shove him, before knocking back into place. "Every Saturday at least, most Fridays or whatever. And every time he would pull over two blocks from my house."

"Uh-oh."

"Yeah. And try to kiss me, and he would unzip his pants and put my hand on it."

"The fucker," Martin says.

"So ugly, the stuff he said. And I would grab, I always remember, the door handle, with the other hand, and I would run out, and down the two blocks thinking he would chase me. He never did. And I would sit on my front yard breathing hard and chewing gum."

"Gum?"

"For my breath. I was in *high school*. And then Monday it would be normal, and the week, and the weekend seeing my friends and it would happen all over again."

It is his cue, Padgett dreads, to say "Why didn't you tell someone?" or "Couldn't you get another ride home?" or "I guess he had a crush on you, it's sort of sad, really."

But Martin just, staring down at his own knees invisible in the woods, says to Padgett, "Well, that's awful."

And, well, it isn't. Not right this second. She lopes her legs down and kicks at something that rolls badly.

"That's my barrel."

"Happy birthday."

She is, he realizes, guessing or joking, or maybe with the cocaine he'd said something. He tilts the barrel upright. "I am in fact thirty today."

"Well," Padgett says, "I bet this is how you planned it."

"You think?"

"Sure, hitting your new decade in a grimy forest. More fun than a barrel."

"Too dark to see the grime," he says.

"Trust me, it's there. You know what I mean, and you know that it is. I'm lost too."

"You sound like a bumper sticker. *Don't follow me—*"

"It's a big con, isn't it?" Her question rattles him in the dark, like an intruder at the door.

"What, life? Not late enough for that conversation."

"Marriage." Her sigh is so long he swears it floats out to sea. "You pretend to be a person and meet another one and they're pretending too. You suit up to be better, kinder, more . . ." Her hands gesture someplace lost in the dark. "And then you get to pretend together, the two of you. You tell a story. Fooling the world while you fool each other. It's the whole thing."

"You sure you're not maid of honor? This would be such a lovely toast."

"That guy fiddling with the special music system. She can't love him like she said, what did she say with the first champagne? *Breathlessly.*"

"He seems nice."

"I'm sure. OK. But then, he is also breathless with her?"

"He's a pudgy guy, probably gets breathless easy."

She laughs and stops. "It's a con. They're tricking each other."

"They're in love."

Padgett is working the spigot. "That's what I mean."

"Hey, that vicar?"

"Yeah."

"Had a blowout with his wife, I mean *fiancée.*"

"Where?"

"Right in the wooden room we were all in."

"I think I meant *why.*"

"Well, this is the thing," Martin says. "He snuck off and had sex with my associate."

"Stanford, really? What kind of sex?"

"The kind," Martin says somewhat patiently, "to which his fiancée strenuously objects."

"Well."

"Yes. And they got in a car. And crashed."

"Is everyone OK?"

"The vicar is gone."

"Dead."

"No one knows, due to goneness. They don't know where he is."

Padgett snorts at this, finishes the cup again. "I don't know where I am either."

"You're in the weird edge of a sort-of forest. Near my bar, I might add."

"Oh yeah? What's it called?"

He tells her and she snorts. "Been open eighteen months. We have a new basement speakeasy space for parties."

"Speakeasy?"

"Well, it's legal. But we're trying to set up a lawbreaking vibe."

Padgett lolls her head back. The mutter of automobiles cross-fades in her drunken ears. "That's very sad to me."

"I think that's half a barrel of cocktails talking."

Padgett drops the cup. They both hear it break, possibly on the barrel. "I haven't talked to my brother in two years."

"Are you just free-associating on sad things now?" Martin stands up, brushes off his pants, and feels the crackle of his finished list in his pocket. It's done. He crossed everything off except the missing barrel, which he now heaves onto his shoulder. "Umph. How'd you even carry this?"

"I didn't. I rolled it."

"You rolled it?"

"A lot spilled out. It was right when I got here. I thought I would need it later."

"You were right about that, I guess."

"That's unlike me."

He leans down but he does not kiss her. Nevertheless, she feels kissed. It's like they're already kissing, or already done doing it. "Come on," he says. "Let's split."

"With you? Split together?"

"Come on."

"Are you inviting me?"

"Pretend I'm falling to my knees. Don't make me abandon you in a forest."

"Are you threatening me?"

"No. I like you, and find myself attracted."

"That," Padgett says, with abrupt sleepiness, "is the same thing." She totters up and watches the slice of the avenue, a horizon broken by thin black trees, seesaw and spin. Her legs are scuffling to walk properly, and then they do, quick learners, stilting her past Martin up through the last of the brush to the sidewalk. It's cold, pretty much. Cars stampede past, the headlights quivering like lousy fireflies. If they notice, these midnight drivers, they do not honk at the man and the woman emerging reckless and restless from the trees. The couple keep walking. The directionless learn by moving, and in the sudden noise of traffic, they're giddy with the sort of jarring joy you can't help, foolishly, trusting absolutely. They go together, the barrel lifted like an infant, new to the world, staring at the crashing sky and wondering what everything is, and where everyone is going.

CHAPTER 2

IT IS ALMOST impossible to be unhappy at Cogwheels, a luxurious and spiritual resort a ways south of San Francisco. Nonetheless, Rachel Nickels has managed it. She's sorry about it, but there it is. Ben, her husband, is next to her in the car, bringing them back. He's wincing, probably at her brittle, forced behavior over the past few days. She doesn't blame him. She wishes she could, though.

The sky above them is blue and white, and the road twists back toward home. On one side is the cliffs—WATCH FOR FALLING ROCKS is the advice of the signs, although what you're supposed to do when rocks are tumbling down upon you is beyond Rachel. Also beyond Rachel is the ocean, clattering below them on the other side, the west coast. Soon enough there will be turnoffs to larger, straighter highways, lined consolingly and claustrophobically with boxy stores and some establishments, shabby and shady-looking, that Rachel wouldn't enter if her life depended on it. Once they hit that highway, the honeymoon will really be over. They will head home, but if they headed east—east and south—they could wind up in Savannah, Georgia, where there is a horse—though surely it is dead—with a very long, floppy neck.

Who knows what this horse is thinking about. The floppy neck is a nightmare, wrinkly and deflated like a gone balloon, giving lie to the comfort that some things can't happen. Someone grabbed that horse's neck with both hands and *pulled*, is what it looked like, downward, and it stretched taffy-like until it just hung there, too much shuddery skin, terrifying. The horse, dead almost certainly now, whatever it is thinking about, could not, it is impossible, be thinking about Rachel Nickels.

But Rachel Nickels has been thinking about the horse, the horse's great shrively neck, all weekend and off and on, mostly on, since she saw this horse when she was eight years old, standing in front of a sweltering hotel before her uncle's wedding and crying at it. This is how she managed unhappiness, piercing and undismissable, at beautiful Cogwheels. The cliffs, the whole area, have historically inspired artists and other bohemian ne'er-do-wells, and Cogwheels is some shined-up version of that story, each room a little tent, draped over heated granite floors, with buttons to press for more towels and salad and coffee grown someplace noble and fair. There is meditation, up a ways, and an infinity pool, open late. The idea is to walk the meadows and lunch on scallops and make love in the tent as the sun goes down, and they've done this. But the sea, spread out beneath them, in its wrinkliness, brought on the thought of the neck, and this terrible horse, galumphing closer and closer across the trampled meadow, to breathe at her and make her feel in her hands its horrifying too-long neck flesh. What could she say? She startled, several times, when her new husband's arms, thick and hairy as the legs of a monstrous horse, wrapped themselves horsily around her on the futon in the tent. It isn't as if, Rachel thinks with her palm on the window, she doesn't know she's ridiculous. Knowing you're ridiculous is, yes, half the battle. But the other half is battling, battling with your ridiculous self.

The car sputters a little. It was the poorest car at Cogwheels, like a filthy hobo among the other guests' shiny machines, silver and black in the valet lot. The place is unaffordable, but Ben Nickels—her *husband*, she married *Ben Nickels* of all people—had got himself a coupon for two free vacation nights at Cogwheels. There were strings attached—only certain days, food and beverage of course not included—but what was a honeymoon if not a vacation with strings attached? Ben and Rachel were married just three months before, and now the music system calls up a song and Ben turns to her and says, "Hey, we like this song," *we*, their opinions locked together like the Electoral College. Oh, she loves him, but sheesh. He is so kind, generous, and very capable at work, with all the little devices and the legal snares they must avoid, and the only man who was properly but not showily horrified when she told him about Jeremy Tyber wrecking her in high school, but how could she tell him about the other shadow, floppy and eternal, that clop-clopped after her? A horse, get over it. But she isn't over it, and she hasn't told him.

She's a fraud, a con artist. Ben thinks he has married Rachel as she has presented herself, a woman, smart and loyal, who through maintenance and worry is just over the midpoint, she estimates, of attractiveness among her female friends, whose work, at the office end of a noble but not whiny nonprofit, looks complementary, next to his bustling, rising tech gig. But he does not know that she, a hack charlatan, did not freely give herself to rolling around in a tent, that she, cranky from little sleep, agreed the view was beautiful, and the trees quiet, but offered no further conversation on the small, mapped hikes because she was haunted by a horse with a big floppy neck. If she had told him this, told *anyone*, she would die an old maid, a muttering spinster shutting the curtains against galloping phantoms. Look at him frowning a little, the car jittering behind a truck so large it has to warn everybody. *If you can't see my mirrors.*

"Work tomorrow," he says. "I don't want this honeymoon to be over."

"I know."

"Let's live there, in the tent."

"Yes," she says.

"You liked it?"

"Of course."

"I was thinking maybe you didn't like it."

"No, no, with you I did."

"I know it was a coupon."

"No, no."

"We could have splurged our credit cards on, I don't know, Paris or something farther."

"No, no. *Ben.*" Across the device she holds his hand a little, on the steering wheel making curves, then rests it on his leg. "It was so lovely."

"Is it a horse? Is it because of a scary horse you saw as a child that you can't quite love me right now?"

But of course he does not ask this. If he did, she'd be too startled to answer, she realizes, and so stops hoping for it.

Instead he takes his eyes off the road for a second. "Shall we stop off at Bottle Grove before home?"

"Oh, that's nice. Yes. Wait. Do you mean the forest or the bar? Or both?"

Ben laughs. "I meant one, but let's do both. A little hike and a little drink and home."

"OK."

"I'll park midway between them."

"Yes, OK."

His eyes stray to his device, and Rachel knows he is thinking that he'll have to lock it up or take it with him when they leave the car. This device is so new, a model hardly available yet and so envied in the quick city. The way he thinks, with his wallet and his head, is for the most part adorable. "Or is it too much trouble?" she asks. "Do you want to get home and shower?"

"No. I mean, if you want." He smiles at her and rewrites it. "Wherever you want. Just, you know, let me come along with you."

She likes this, and he takes her hand and she likes this too. He has said this before, that he just wants to be with her. Tag along, is how he put it at the beginning. Go with. Go anywhere with. Stay with. Marry me, just take me with you.

They're in San Francisco quick. Bottle Grove is hardly out of the way, particularly if they're going there. The highway leads easily to the boulevard, and the music device slips into Ben's windbreaker like a baby kangaroo, what do they call them? The jacket rustles against her arm, and under the eyes of the Masonic temple they walk the few blocks into the forest.

They were just here, getting married in the grove, and now they're here, married. They go in together, not very far. The wind waits; probably some creatures are someplace, waiting, too. *Joeys*, is what they call them, Rachel remembers now, those little hopping things.

"It was a lovely wedding," Ben says, as formally as a guest. "Until, I mean."

Rachel thinks of the fight, the wife with the cinematic hairdo and the vicar who officiated, however he slipped away. Blood on the tires, but that was just something, likely untrue, she heard later from a breathless friend. The sentimental journey is less a success now. "Let's not fight like that," she says. "Like they did. It should be a reminder, the scene they made."

"We won't," Ben says. "We wouldn't. Ever."

"Let's just remember not to. Screaming at each other. Oh, Ben, it was so sad to me. You know?"

"So we won't."

"But really."

"Really," Ben says, putting an end to it. "We won't."

But of course, Rachel knows, they will. You stand in a field and marry someone and one day, many days, scream at them harder than you have ever, at anyone. She looks at all the eucalyptus, standing together like co-workers at a party. They're together now; she has lost, what would you call it, her by-herselfness, and gained this man squinting toward one of the trees. A little of her life has been taken, misplaced in his pocket, like when she was on an airplane and misplaced a pair of sunglasses, and so many years later those sunglasses have yet to be found. The breeze moves on through. The path twists over. Ben steps past her to the tree he is frowning at and plucks from the leaves and bark a long feather, very long and gray, and waves it at her smiling, quills it around in the air like the Founding Fathers. It is almost impossible to be unhappy looking at him here. "The tree grows feathers!" he says. "It's the only explanation."

"Let's not tell anyone," she says. "We'll start a company!"

"By our first anniversary we'll have a bird of our own that we made ourselves, and then we'll take it public. Look, here's another one!"

He hands this one to Rachel and she whirls around with it. The trees, the whole place, whirls with her. It's a little foolish, a little freeing. A goof, a talisman. Keep horses away. Keep us married, keep him fooled about how I am really. I will try, like these trees breathing and showering down two more feathers, to be a spell of breathless enchantment, even, especially, when I want to tear my own eyes out and cannot sleep from trouble. Let this nice giggling man shade me from my worries and cares and I'll try, once a week minimum, to do the same. Another one, a small handful on the ground. Rachel grabs as many as she can see and confettis them like the end of the war, and then mid-toss she rounds a bush and there is the rest of the carcass, a crater of blood and feathers and more blood and a terrible gray-yellow bird foot of spikes.

"Eek," Rachel says, but not a shriek; she just says it. "Yikes."

"Well," Ben says, and then tries to sort of nudge at it, as if anything looking like that could still be alive. "Well, that's awful. Poor thing."

"Yeah."

"Let's get a drink," her husband says. "I meant Bottle Grove the bar, all along."

They start to trudge out. "It's jinxed now," Rachel says. "Our wedding spot."

"Kind of jinxed anyway."

"Because of Reynard."

Ben scuffles his shoes. "No, not that. I didn't want to tell you until after the wedding. My old girlfriend—"

"Tina with the hair?"

"The other one."

"OK."

"She killed a guy's dog here."

"What?"

"She had this dog when we lived together. We had it, I guess. It was grandfathered in. Hyacinth. About this big."

He does not remember, Rachel realizes, that she's seen this dog. "That's not big."

Her husband smiles. "About this small, then. And she used to walk it in Bottle Grove, not very often. Anyway, some big dog attacked her—"

"The dog?"

"The dog, yes. Her dog was attacked by this other dog, and she killed it."

"The big dog."

"With a big knife," Ben says. "She carried it with her."

"Your ex-girlfriend carried around a big knife? She killed a dog and you still went out with her?"

"Just a few more months," Ben says. "It really rattled me. But you were so happy to have the wedding here—"

"Darling."

"—that I just buried it. But yeah, that's the part that sticks with me too. That it happened, and I stayed."

"Yeah."

"But who knows why people stay together, right?"

Rachel almost yanks back her hand, but then offers it again. Ben slaps his own head.

"I didn't mean it like that," he says.

"It was perfect, the way you said it," she says, and as they walk out of the forest, she feels very safe indeed, to be together in the streets.

Blocks away, the bar's just opened—literally, the door has just swung open. "Late, but I made it," Martin says to Padgett, and it is not clear if he is apologizing. Bottle Grove opens at four—it's ten after, now—and Padgett has been waiting since three something, leaning against the sun-spattered parking meters feeling lonely and addicted. She's the only one who shows up at four who doesn't work there, aside from a woman, not old enough to be an old lady, who shows up, lipstick messy, and orders champagne, very cold. A ridiculous request, Padgett thinks, because the champagne is in a fridge, cold as it's ever going to get. Now that Martin has come she feels she is still waiting, but for what, she can't decide. "How was your day?"

"Wasteful," she says, already sitting on the stool.

"Did you—"

"I didn't do anything."

He walks toward her, suddenly, at least to her, wearing just one shoe and on the other foot a sock so filthy it might not be black. "It was caught in the escalator," he says, raising his leg.

"What?"

"I took BART to have coffee with my brother." BART is what they call the train—Bay Area Rapid Transit, although

Padgett can never believe that's the real name—but this is the first she's heard about a brother. "On the escalator going home the shoe got caught. I had to move fast so it wasn't my foot. It ate the whole thing up. They gave me an address to write them, and maybe I'll get a check."

"It ate up your shoe? I've never heard of that."

"Neither had anyone at the BART station. Although they said last year a barefoot girl lost a toenail."

"Well," Padgett says, "*barefoot*."

"Yes, but walking around with one sock's not better. I don't have a lot of shoes and these, this one, is, are, probably my favorites. They better pay."

"Yeah," Padgett says, and then neither of them says what is obvious to know, which is that Bay Area Rapid Transit is not going to buy Martin Icke a shoe. The only job he's ever had that wasn't bartending was an office job, do-goody, and three weeks in, the boss told him to take a box of crucial files outside and lock it in her car, which she had left unlocked a block away. Turns out there were two cars unlocked on that block, both ratty and a little hip such as might be owned by his boss. Martin didn't know make, didn't know model. It could happen to anyone, maybe, but it didn't. It happened to Martin, and now Martin is happening to her.

They are still, since that wedding, together, and that's weird. Isn't it? The night they rolled out the barrel, they'd ended up first at another bar, a dingy place with one TV for news and the other one for football, and poured everyone a shot of the Happy Couple. They had more drinks, a strategy they keep employing. They left the barrel behind and took to the sidewalks, very late and still dirty from scuffing around the grove. They kept each other from stumbling because they were both stumbling, so by all appearances stumbling was just a way to walk. They didn't kiss until a red light and a busy street forced them to lean against a sign announcing that the bus no longer stopped there. "I want to fuck you," he said against her mouth, "so *badly*," and that night he did, very badly, and until daylight they listened to records and smoked and, Padgett tries to think, no, that's it. His apartment was not filthy but it was small, with shelves of strange liquors bird-dogged by friends on far-flung retreats, and some angry books about what was wrong, politically mostly, with every-thing. He didn't have room for a dog, or even a cat, or a space where she could keep more than a handful of clothes. The only thing he had room for was improvement. She had learned that if you were seventy-five cents short for cigarettes and yogurt at the corner store, or six dollars, he would likely leave you hanging, spacing out at the beef jerky with his hands in his dusty pockets.

But he is kind, or kind of kind. He cannot walk by the paltriest lemonade stand without treating the flushed propri-etor like a professional, buying two cupfuls he then improves with flask whiskey when he rounds the corner with Padgett. The drinks are delicious. They have them until late, and then hit dawn with cheerful regret for a greasy breakfast. It is hard for Padgett to figure out precisely or even partially what she is doing here, on a stool that's now basically designated hers, watching him, one-footed and frowning at a sip of coffee and slicing limes. The sex is still mostly out of the way, relegated beneath the strong drinks and the short, pausey conversations. Their occasional lusty bouts of romanticism are like a car alarm in the neighborhood, just sometimes piping up. Mostly they just lounge around, he in the same tie he hasn't untied for days, just loosened and hung on a nail, and her doing whatever it is she's doing at the bar. She recognizes the look she keeps catching him giving her, *romantic* would be the word, a little feverish from a bug he's caught worse than she has. He has big plans that probably won't pan out. She has no plans and that will likely work out just that way. Oh, she doesn't know. Martin puts a drink in front of her.

"Sip it," he says. "Charging eleven dollars each."

"Seems steep."

"Yeah, but we make the ginger ale."

"How does one," she says, "make ginger ale?"

"Sugar mostly," Martin says. "Story of the world." He keeps looking at her, the way he looks at the building she lives in. Padgett, over and over, shoos him away from even a few questions about her family, but once, after downing Old-Fashioneds from every spot on Divisadero, she was so goopy she didn't notice he sat next to her in the backseat as a phone-fetched car dropped her off in a comfortable, view-soaked neighborhood where absolutely nobody he knows lives. Or will ever live. Padgett has her own place, but just techni-cally; her own entrance in her mother's crumbly—well, it's a *mansion*, its ugliness does not disqualify it from that tag. He was right the first time: she's rich. A rich dame. The Bottle family, who donated the grove he snitched for the name of the bar. Since then, he has the feeling, not that they fit together, but that something, some task, could be done with them both in tandem, whisk and muffin tin, paint can and mortgage, shovel and terrified witness.

"It's good," she tells him, re the drink.

"Good for a boys' night out?"

"Oh yeah, your speakeasy party tonight."

He makes a gesture like she won a stuffed animal. "You should stick around."

"I'm not invited."

"I just did. You're the barman's girl."

Padgett rattles the straw in the ice, and from inside the dark room, through the doorway's bright, bright rectangle, she looks out at the neighborhood. There's a passerby passing by: a small child new at walking, its legs stilted stilts. Then a pause, then the toddler's mother, pushing a stroller with a baguette in it, like it's the bread she really loves best. This, Padgett thinks, is what she's up against. "I'm your girl?"

Martin is frowning at something else. "I should," he says, "wear two shoes for this thing tonight. My lucky boots, I guess. Once Stanford comes and everything's set up downstairs—"

"Give me your key," she says, "and tell me where you keep your lucky boots."

He looks at her and her drink, almost finished. His keys are chained to him on a ring. One of his fingers, just one, drums the bar.

"Forget it," she says.

"No."

"Just offering."

"I know it was just weird, I made it weird."

"That you don't trust me with your keys, yes, is weird, Martin."

"Padgett, you're—" But then the sentence appears to be over.

"I'm," she agrees, and this is another time when it could have all gone up, like arson, instead of fizzling off. This sort of moment has happened, Padgett would offhand guess, four times in the last two weeks. Customers arrive.

"You open?" Ben asks.

"Hey," the barman says, halfway heartily. "How's married life?"

"Extremely—" Ben says, "delightful."

"Normal," Rachel says. "We're just back from our honeymoon, actually."

Padgett drains her glass and slides into this weird narrow bench they have in the corner, by the jukebox. They're all she needs, these people, the almost last straw.

"That honeymoon was *lengthy*," Martin says approvingly.

"No, we waited," Ben says. "Couldn't get away until this weekend."

"Cogwheels," Rachel says. "Beautiful."

Martin pours the drinks and Ben looks grateful. "Welcome home and drink up," he says. "Private party tonight. Taste the fixings."

Ben looks around, spots a pouting shroud in a corner bench. "A private party *here*?"

"It's not unthinkable. Downstairs."

"Oh, right," Rachel says. "Your speakeasy thing."

"My speakeasy thing. We got a big client, be proud of me."

"I *am* proud," Rachel says, actually kind of proudly.

Ben is looking at his wife. "You know about this?"

"He's talked about it for months," Rachel says, knocking a thumb at Martin, and she sips. "Ooh. It's your ginger ale."

"Artisanal ginger ale, cheap whiskey, lemon bitters," Martin says, but Rachel is reminding her husband.

"When you had that big project, working late, I hung out here sometimes, that's how I found them for the wedding."

"Right," Ben says, and Martin says it too: "The wedding."

The room gets quiet for the car crash, the missing vicar, blood on the trees. Padgett brings her drink to a slurpy finish but nobody, she is grateful, cranes to recognize the substitute they got stuck with at the last minute. Instead they talk about Cogwheels, the tents, the cliffs. The ocean rippling like skin. Rachel finishes her drink with a half shudder. "One more?" Martin offers. "Then I should throw you out, probably."

"OK?" Ben checks with her.

"The drinks are good," Rachel says, pretending she has to be nudged into drinking more.

"Variation on an old classic," Martin says, "called the Horse's Neck," and the couple is gone in seconds, first Rachel and then, confused and fumbling too much cash into Martin's hand, the husband. Martin frowns after them, knowing it was something he said but not knowing what, not an uncommon confusion for him. The barman tilts out the couple's glasses and the ice slithers into the sink. "Come out, come out, wherever you are."

"I'm right here," Padgett says, slouchily.

"Can I tell you a thing? Those, Ben and Rachel there, are customers, and if you were nice to them—"

"I don't work here, Martin. They're not my customers."

"I was more saying it as a general sort of approach to things."

"I don't really *approach* things," Padgett reminds him, but she has in fact walked to the bar, to show Martin her empty tumbler. A piece of ice crackles in her mouth.

"Yeah, but."

"Martin, when I want advice, you will know it, because the world will have ended."

"You could just be, to my friends at least, a little, I'm going to say *warmer*."

"They're not your *friends*."

"OK, but—"

"You just said *customers*."

He does not say that customers are friends if you're at work, if your work is not booming, if you owe a lot of goddamn money. She's too rich to get that, probably. Martin just looks at her, the blending of two old San Francisco families, and wonders, as with the mansion, the best way to get in, or maybe he should just keep walking. But he doesn't say anything.

She looks at him as if saying the sentence, "Pour me another and leave me alone," and he does, he does. The drink has a sharp taste but a calming texture, all the soft threads of ginger like a loose ghost in the bubbles. She sips it, two strong sips, and feels the walls of the bar shimmer as if in a breezy breeze.

"Stay for the party," he says quietly.

"Put some music on."

Martin holds up a device. "I have to set up his network."

"A speakeasy party and they don't want the jukebox? What kind of lousy, no-good—"

"It's a *party*," Martin says, more or less patiently, "for this new music system. The Vic is relaunching it, or reworking it, or anyway, it's happening, or trying to happen again. So he asked me, through an underling with a very large party budget, to hook up the Vic's system for the Vic's party. This is sort of what I mean."

"Your *meaning*," Padgett said, "is now determined by some mogul's—"

"Stop it. It's music for a party. I am hoping, yes, to make a success of the speakeasy. The Vic having a party here is huge."

"The Vic, the Vic, the Vic." This is a rallying cry lately in San Francisco, of people tired of the mogul, of all the moguls, although it is a rallying cry made weaker by Padgett saying it while tipping her glass down to her mouth, ice cubes smacking her nose.

Martin leans over the bar and removes the glass from her premises. "That's two already," he says. "Slow down. Slow down and stay."

"Why," Padgett says, "should I?"

His eyes get bright, or maybe, Padgett thinks, he's always, maybe, brighter than she thinks. He can't say, or doesn't know how to, that he's falling harder and harder for Gail Padgett Bottle, so he just says, "I have plans."

Padgett is back on her stool, twirling around. The stool does not actually twirl, so she has to do it herself. "I don't," she admits. "I have no plans for the evening or anything."

"Invite a friend to join in. There will be a lot of booze and wealth."

"My friends are kind of in a holding pattern," she says, and stops twirling so she is facing the wall. A poster makes her miss, miss, miss her brother. The barman leans farther over to take her shoulders and move her to face him. It's a bulky maneuver, like lifting a rocking chair.

"I have plans," he says again, and Padgett guesses she would say his eyes are twinkly. Her own eyes want to cry just looking at him. She closes them instead and kisses him, first just for something to do and then, like it is with the two of them, lengthily.

"Stop messing around," Stanford says cheerily in the doorway. "You have time to lean, you have time to clean."

"If you have time to think," Padgett says, "you have time to drink."

Martin tosses Stanford a towel. "You have time to duck—"

Padgett laughs. Stanford pats her shoulder hello. "Where are we on being ready?"

"Almost," Martin says, his fingers dialing on the device. A gravelly man says soothingly, over strings and drums, that this song goes out to all those who have seen trouble. Padgett thinks that's nice of him, to dedicate the tune to her like that.

"Enough ginger ale?"

"Plenty," Martin says, the list out of his pocket. "Limes done. Downstairs basically set."

"What are those vodka boxes on the floor?"

"Something I should put away, like a grown-up."

Stanford puts his palms together, so much lighter than the rest of him. "Let's make some money tonight."

"They paid us already," Martin says. "My phone just told me it cleared."

"Let's make some let's-have-nine-more-parties-here kind of money."

"I hear that," Martin says, and takes a corkscrew from the counter to scratch his back with. Stanford opens a closet and slides out a little blackboard, hinged like a crooked tent, where he likes to write little sidewalk slogans. *It's five o'clock some-where. Come in and tell us about it. This gin won't drink itself. No-shows welcome.* His handwriting is arty, so many serifs and curlicues it's hardly language. *Private party* is what it will say. "Slip me a coffee," he says, with a handful of chalk.

Martin is just pouring his down the sink. "Bad today."

"This is the last bastion of bad coffee in San Francisco," Padgett says. "You should be proud."

Stanford has reached back into the closet, and his hand comes out rattling a little red plastic cup, a frat boy dice game. Padgett watches him tip it and palm something. "This'll do," he says, and yanks his head back like a baby bird before passing a pill to Martin, and then, after very brief consideration, to Padgett. It's white and oval, with no marking she can discern in the dim light.

"What is this?"

"Calcium," Stanford says. "Women your age, with your brittle bones—"

"Sorry I asked," Padgett says, and swallows it dry. The singer, too, bemoans his regrets.

"You look good," Stanford says to her. "Good for a party."

"I guess that pill is working already."

Martin shoulders a rack of glasses and pushes a box of paper napkins to Padgett. Eventually everything gets used up. She doesn't work here, but here she is. She has her own place, in a fading family home, and her own purse, full of fading family money. But she has no plans. So she follows Martin down a metal spiral staircase, the biggest corkscrew in the bar, to the speakeasy basement. It's not an impressive place, but they've improved it, with a large wooden table Vikings might feast at and heavy iron curtain rods with heavy closed drapes where the windows would be in the windowless room. Little speakers keep the song going in the air, and Martin unpacks the glasses in sort of rhythm on the second bar, a flourishy, antlered thing hauled from a flea market by Stanford. Martin doesn't ask Padgett to do anything with the napkins, like arrange them, and she doesn't, merely thunks them on the table.

"Until the guests show," Martin says, with a quick glance at his father's wristwatch, "you're the only woman who's been down here."

"That's the most romantic-slash-creepy thing—" but two more women clitter-clatter down the staircase, spoiling the statistic.

"We're early," says one, and the other says, "I'm Shandra." Their dresses are tight-fitting and short both ways, the sort that always remind Padgett of a costume she wore when she was a kid, of a tube of toothpaste. Of course, she also had a paper chef's hat for the cap, and these women just have makeup, so glittery in the diminished light it looks like masks. They are miles from the aloof corporate glamour she'd made up in her head about this party. "Be with you in a minute, ladies," Martin says, all gallantry and coasters.

"Who are you?" says the one who isn't Shandra, like Padgett is something she's found in that tiny purse. Padgett says she's Padgett. "Can I get a rickey then?"

"Can I get a rickey? Can I get a rickey too?"

"She doesn't work here," Martin calls out, and the women look her over again. Padgett knows, she's pretty sure, that these women are not hookers, but they seem like the type who would squeal, and not slap you, if you asked them, which is maybe worse.

"Sorry," the woman says now. "I always think everyone's a server. Ask Shandra."

"*So true*," Shandra says. "Are you into fashion? You look like that."

Padgett adjusts her sleeve. The sweater she is wearing, and has worn for five days, she snitched from her mother one day when it got colder. "I'm really jazzed about it," the woman insists, not evidently joking, or maybe so deadpan she's even meaner than she seems, a seventh-grade birthday party all over again. The chemicals, with the pill and two drinks, are drifting everything apart. Padgett says, "It's time for a drink," and the women nod and say *definitely* in spooky unison.

"Tonight's special is our version of a classic, the Horse's Neck," Martin says, "with Hallowed Spirits whiskey—"

"*Rickeys*," Shandra says, suddenly a toucan. "Rickeys! Rickeys!"

Padgett cannot help admiring the way Martin does not, in the slightest, give them a sigh. "I'm betting you ladies have a special way—"

"Hot Fox Vodka with agave syrup, two limes, and soda," Shandra says, just as new guests spiral down, already wild-eyed, already shouting like seagulls for bread, "Can I get a—? Can I get a—?" Padgett slinks off, or stalks off—anyway, she's across the room, trying not to cover her ears, and in no time things are in full swing. Martin's face is flushed. Stanford is moving like a modern dancer, grabbing empties as the Vic's songs segue, cross-fade, pause. The room is sweaty but maybe that's just Padgett's hands. Each cuff link is sarcastic, every hooded sweatshirt sincere. It's not a lot of people, maybe thirty, with the men—*boys*, really, hardly anyone's much older than Padgett—clapping each other, almost folk-dancy, on toned-up shoulders and arms and even faces, the women all dressed as if for a different scenario, set in a nightclub, their occasional bustiers all chainy like a comic book Amazon. Padgett thinks they could be girlfriends or maybe just in Human Resources. They certainly appear to be for hire. What they are all talking about Padgett does not know, due to not listening, due to not giving a fuck. Now and then, and now, Stanford hands her another fizzy drink and the pill continues to meander through her system like a tapeworm, hitting her neck, her shoulders, her teeth and eyes—and then she snaps to, facing the face of an unknown man.

"What about sports?" he has just finished saying, apparently.

"What about them?"

"Do you like them? It's your turn to talk, I've been talking."

Has he? "Have you?"

He leans in with a frown, over the music. "Do I what?"

"Like," Padgett says, inventing a parlor game of starting a sentence not knowing how she'll finish it up. "To. Drink. Beer. At the. Stadium."

"And *how*," the guy says. "I *knew* you were OK. You don't work the same place the girls do."

"What," Padgett says. "Is. That. Place."

"Exactly," the man says. "They should all have robot voices like that. I'm glad I tried you. I mean, there must be thousands of people in the world, right? And you like *baseball*."

Has she said that? "But I *don't*," she says, ready, *eager* even, to explain she should not be trusted, anything out of her mouth.

"Most women who like baseball are—" The man extends both hammy arms to her like he's passing her a bowling ball, and then widens his hands away from her hips to describe the size of a woman unacceptable to him, about his build, actually. "What is it with fat women and baseball?"

She would give up anything for the power to summon a plague of snakes to venom this man, all of them, to death. Across the room, Martin sees her, cocks an eyebrow meaning, what, she can't guess. Something on his list. She tries to glare back the sentence *Why are you leaving me here*, too much for one glare. "I'm trying," she says. "To learn. To take. Things. As compliments."

"That's good," he says. "It wasn't like this in tech when I started out. In the beginning San Francisco was the Wild West. Everyone was starting up without starting out. There was a place we used to drink, where we loaded up before going off to ski on weekends, a place untamed, you know? Every week the crowd grew bigger and soon we all read in the newspaper that you-know-who were talking about buying the whole bar, hook and barrel, so they didn't have to share. I would try to remember everything I eavesdropped and sneak into the bathroom to write it all out on my little new phone . . ." He continues to talk affectionately about life in certain nearby valleys, and she just stares at things on and near him which hold briefly her fierce and offhand fascination. Someone in this room, she thinks, reads newspapers?

"Have you heard of the Kitsune School?"

The drink, pressed against her face, is not cool enough. "I haven't heard of anything."

"He changed the name after his dear departed, which is either nice or creepy, right? I know I sound cynical, but if you knew the troubles I've seen."

"Dear departed what?"

He gives her the frown of *Give me a break.* "Wife. The mother of his child, and she died in childbirth, if you can believe it or not, in this day and age. The lives of these times, right? She was *passionate*, everyone says, about early education, so the Vic founded—well, he purchased a school. Then gave money to run it, to her old roommate, a pet project. Ariel Park, she's over there with those two horribles. Kitsune, named after her. Japanese for fox, as if there isn't enough—"

It, something, makes her shiver, the pill probably, a shadow over something. "The Vic's," she tries, "wife's name was Fox?"

The man is irked. She is not listening raptly enough to him. Padgett's last real boyfriend had that problem with her too. "*Maureen.* How can you not know this? I thought this is all required for any SF citizen. The *baby* is Kitsune. Maureen read a lot of those Japanese comic books, you know what I mean? She was Japanese, I mean the sort of Japanese where you grow up in Vancouver. You really don't know this? Beautiful baby, Kitsune. Citizen of the world. Somebody said the Vic has actual Maori in him, if he does, it shows in her. Ten bucks says she'll be on the cover of some ad campaign, some noble effort, in his name. God I sound terrible, but this is where we are. I saw the radio thing on those hikers who got kidnapped in Bolivia, and you know what they said was their mistake? Not having a good enough map. Eighteen months imprisoned. A good enough map."

Padgett feels like the barefoot girl in the train station with her lost, eaten toenail. She holds up a finger. The guy stops in the middle of his trip to Baja. "You got bathroom to go to? I'm monopolizing, aren't I?"

"*Monotonizing*," she corrects, and waterbeds her feet across the room to pull, can't make it work, *push* the door with a silhouette wearing an upside-down triangle for a dress. She looks back at the big man, still yakking, and goes in. The light's pink, bad. Someone else's turd is in the bowl like a manatee. No privacy, no space for her. She pees on top of it and splashes water on her face, a droplet on her ear in her reflection, hanging like jewelry. She looks harder into the mirror.

How've you been, Bottle?

There are no paper towels, due to carbon and the environment, blares the sign over the blower. She holds her face under too. So loud and so hot, and in the rush she realizes it has been a test, a pranky test. This, the yakking man, is the Vic she's been talking to. Of course it is, of course he was. This is the movie star in the airport bar being told he looks familiar, Zeus in a peasant cloak playing trickster, *I'm Gatsby, thought you knew, old sport.* She's been played, conned out. She smiles at it, and when the fan offs automatically, the speakeasy music has switched—someone screwed up the playlist, it makes her snort—over to a man, talking in even, lively tones about the mind-body problem.

She creeps the door open and there is the Vic, on the staircase like a Caesar, and to her disapproval—for what *that's* worth—he's had his baby brought to the bar, the fox he was bragging about, right next to him in a bundle bound to the chest of, of course, a male nanny, looking maybe twenty years old in a hooded top with the name of a band she actually sort of likes. It is he who is talking, earnestly, or at least a show of earnestly, and why, how drunk is everyone, to let the nanny make a toast? With a tall ginger glass he finishes hands up with "That's what I'm talking about!" and the room goes nuts with cheers and claps and the baby cries and everyone awws and the baby cries harder and everyone laughs. To Padgett it feels like a pagan sacrifice, like the baby will be devoured at the Viking table by Shandra and the other vixen harpies. But instead the music just comes back on and Padgett steadies herself. The poor baby. First chapter of a bitter memoir, right there. Alarmingly, the nanny heads down the twisty stairs right toward her, one hand holding his drink and the other holding the baby close.

"You missed it," he says. "I saw you sneak to the bathroom right when I arrived."

"You're sweet to notice."

"I *never* get ducked out on. It makes me curious."

"Don't be."

"I mean, everybody wants the speech."

She looks at him, familiar now with his eyebrows raised from magazine articles she always skips. Behind his head the yakker waggles his eyebrows. Martin is laughing and looking down at his list on the bar, and Padgett has the feeling, uneasy but not disasteful, that this was what he meant by the plan.

"*You're* Vic. *The Vic.*"

He bows a little, toward the baby. Father, not nanny. Billionaire, not undergrad. This is San Francisco, is where it is, she thinks, and then stops thinking a bit.

"Your turn now to say your name," he says. "That's how we're doing it this year."

"Padgett."

"Padgett. As in the Padgetts who—

"Friend of the bartender," she says, "or something."

"Maybe you could buy him another shoe."

"You noticed that."

"I'm like that." The Vic is not even cracking a smile but his eyes are all tinsel. "I noticed you and I'm still noticing. The bartender makes good drinks, though. I'm glad my spies noticed him for me." He sips through the straw and then, over the baby, tilts it to Padgett so she can sip too, and recite the recipe.

"Artisanal ginger ale, cheap whiskey, lemon bitters."

"I'll have you know," the Vic says, "that Hallowed Spirits whiskey is *my* company."

"Oops."

"Yeah."

"OK, but to be fair you own *everything*."

He pushes a place on his nose that, in a few years, will be holding up his glasses. "Bored of that," he says, "all the rich jokes."

"That must be very tough. Is your plane fancy?"

"You know," he says, "it really is."

"Good. I'd hate to buy a plane and then it's just an old van in the sky that needs reupholstering."

"I was just in it a few hours ago."

"Where did it take you?"

"Overseas. I had to oversee something."

"China? Little kids not soldering the wires quick enough?"

"I don't touch hardware. Amsterdam. And no, I didn't smoke anything. And you know what?"

Padgett has to bite her tongue instead of saying, as she would to her brother, "Chicken butt," and then wonders why she is bothering. "I don't know," she answers out loud.

"I think they were conning me. We would talk and they would confer, and I swear it was so gibberishy I have decided Dutch is not a real language, just fakey words in no order. What do you say to that?"

"As the Dutch say," Padgett punchlines for him, "*jicama blowjob peanut.*" They talk like this for a while, so it is seeming. She leans in and out of being plastered, while the Vic just pats the sleeping baby and pokes his ice. She can't decide if she's flirting with him or kicking his ass. Shandra flits in on her way out and kisses Padgett, what the fuck was that, on the cheek. Three songs, or maybe the same song, take up the idea that women ought to get nasty on the dance floor, and then stop.

"Ladies and gentlemen!" Martin is megaphoning through his legal pad folded into a sloppy cone. Padgett is the only woman left in the room. "This is a raid! It is two in the morning, and the law says you must leave the speakeasy."

"The speakeasy's kowtowing to the law?" asks a fratty guy, to general chucklery.

"The Vic *is* the law in this town," shouts another one.

"We are turning on the lights," Martin continues, his voice old-timey through the cone. "Advise your eyes."

Padgett wants to leave before she's squinting. She is just steadying for a sec before the treacherous climb up the staircase when a hand stops hers on the banister. Across the room, Martin is grinning like she's shouted *"Bingo!"* and makes, as all boys make, a gun out of his cocked finger. He pulls the trigger and Padgett's eyes follow the imaginary path of the invisible bullet to the young, wide face of the Vic, handsome with money and babydom and a confident, bolted smile.

"I'll walk you out," the Vic tells her. "Let me walk you out."

She takes him with her, or vice versa, spiraling up through the staircase as the lights go on beneath them. The rest of the night and the early morning are a slow strobe, items on a shuffled list Padgett can't quite read or make sense of. They arrive at a house that is gray and glass on the outside and polished wood everywhere in the interior. The car is stupidly fancy, a midlife crisis too early. The baby—Kitsune, she remembers—gets strapped in and then so does Padgett, the seat belt impressive as a cosmonaut's, thick, with a buckle right over her breastbone. She can't get in, then she can't get out. She appears to be leaving a party with a famous man, or has left the party already, the moon mooning across the view of big bright storage blocks on carrier ships at rest in the Bay. It's a high-up neighborhood where it's no big deal, with lawyers, to snatch up three houses from immigrant families and make one boxy glass home for yourself.

The baby is handed over to someone who may or may not have called her *Miss*. Padgett stands on a porch, is what it is, and tries to find the Golden Gate Bridge, her bearings, on this balcony. The Vic is talking about water and says the word *restoration*. She sits on a bench in the kitchen that looks too new to be restored, but he means the water, the oxygen in the water, fizzy and iceless, that cools down her throat and, she sees this with her hands on the sheets of the bed, lifts the flush away from her skin.

The music has shifted, of course. How could it not shift perfectly in the home of the king of the system? He is standing over her, extremely naked, his hand on his own genitals like he's afraid she's going to kick him. Her sweater is draped over a barstool at the kitchen counter that she tricks him into admitting was the priciest kind. She has seen them, lined up in a store south of Market: the ones so cheap they were already malfunctional, the OK ones, the built-to-last ones such as Martin and Stanford have purchased, the upper-middle-class ones for new condos, and then the barstools so pricey it fills her with shame for the species. If she opens her eyes, which she keeps not doing, she can see all the way up his downy legs, not a flattering view but an arousing one, vulnerable and full of hair. You don't have to do anything, when you go home with a man, if you let a man take you home. Except, Padgett thinks, basically you do. So she takes her clothes off, and his face just *lights up*, something she sees in him for weeks, and this, she thinks—*this* must be the plan, too.

The sky's blue, a perfect gray blue from the bed. It's the morning, the baby kicking in a little chair with sweet potato on its—*her*—mouth and she, Padgett, the coffee not strong enough, is standing in this miracle of an enormous kitchen. She does not check her phone but he has two, maybe three, and when he slips out to the balcony to talk to someone, making faces through the glass at the baby, she patters to the freezer at the far end and finds vodka, Polish and grassy-tasting, to gobble from her coffee cup, and she falls asleep in the bed again while he showers, waking after some jolty dream to his body leaning onto hers. He smells like pretentious soap. This time she does say no, citing the baby, although the baby has been taken someplace again. More vodka while he shaves, then he sits cross-legged in boxer shorts on the bed and asks her if she's ever heard of, been to, a place called Cogwheels.

"I grew up in California," she says. "My mom had a yoga protégé when I was twelve and we went there for his birthday. Or, hold on, maybe mine."

"I want to take you there for the weekend."

Padgett cannot remember what day it is. It apparently makes her look reluctant.

"Don't look at it that way. It's not a huge deal. My company has a plan."

"What company? What plan?"

"They use my music. My music users get some discounts."

"Oh, so you won't have to pay much, Boy Billionaire. *That's* a relief."

"I need to meet them a little this weekend. But we could make a weekend out of it."

"What's the catch?"

The Vic laughs and stands up and starts with T-shirts and belts. "Eventually, the catch is that everyone will need to buy all the music all over again and pay me for doing it. It's not going to be how it was. Songs, musicians, it's just *on* now, like water from a tap. And the money's in whose faucet it is."

Padgett cannot get over what not a genius he is, how his ideas are just phrases with a cute face. "I meant, what's the catch for me?"

"Oh."

"Not for content utilizers in the world's quadrants."

"I just thought you would like it. Someplace fine." He plops down on the bed again and flares back the sheet from her body. He is looking at her like an onscreen search, scrolling for the right hit. His fingers are holding her near the knees, fairly nonsexually, like he can check a pulse or chakra or whatever she has in her besides vodka and a feeling of falling behind. What is it, she thinks, he sees in her, what is he seeing? "You're the first one," he says, his hands moving up to hold her ass in two places, "since Maureen died."

The baby's so little. Died in childbirth, was what that talky man said. "No, I'm not."

"Well, you're the first I've liked." He puts the heel of his palm between her legs and she raises her hips a little, like she's taking pants off, ready to say yes. But she only says yes to the weekend, and he hoodies up and leaves. She has one more drink and a shower, moves a toothpasted finger around in her mouth. She calls up a map on her phone and the map calls up a car to get her home, and the weekend is postponed four times but then happens, the way economists will say, over and over, that the economy is terrible, and one day nobody has any money.

It is almost impossible to be unhappy there. Padgett certainly doesn't manage it. The private lessons in some stretchy form of meditation, the orgasms in the breezy tent, the goat cheese with nettles nestled into it, conspire to make her smiley. And a lot of wine. The road back is like a listing ship, after two mimosas at brunch and then a swig, two of them, deep and wide, while the Vic was loading their duffels, from a bottle of chardonnay that was just sitting there in the little lobby cabin in a weeping ice bucket. Swerving, yes. The sky's dizzying. But she feels happy, a grin on her face like she's tightroping, and although she keeps waiting for the feeling to leave, it. Just. Doesn't.

"I had a really nice time," says the Vic.

There's music on, electric guitars churning like someone's drawing Padgett a bath. No need to speak.

"And I liked meeting your mom, when I picked you up. She mentioned your brother?"

"I don't," Padgett says, "talk about anything about him."

"I'm sorry about that."

At this Padgett blinks open. "You are?"

"Sure," Vic says, just a few fingers on the steering wheel. "The whole point is to be as vulnerable as possible for as long as possible."

"Where did you hear that?"

"All over the place, everybody knows that. We should be telling each other things."

Things. Out under the window there are workers on the side of the road, huddled together, poking with sticks. What is anyone doing?

The Vic sighs at the gear shift. "If you could meet me maybe somewhere halfway."

"Vic," Padgett says, realizing she almost said *the.* "I can't meet you halfway. I can barely meet you, I've barely *met* you. You are very famous—"

"Stop."

"And *grieving.*"

"Grieving?"

"Your wife died. I think you're in shock or this is, I am, some shocky rebound."

"That's not what it is."

"That's what it always is, with a spouse when the other spouse, who is your *wife*, dies. I don't know you! I'm along for the ride but I can't pretend to . . ." The rest of the sentence is plucked away by white wine.

"Let me tell you a thing," the Vic says, and then he does: a story about a dog.

She blinks along with it, watching herself fall for him falling for her, and the story, too, she's falling for, she can tell.

"That's sad," she admits when the story's over, but her mind is straining to rub the fog off the mirror. She doesn't skip the magazine articles anymore, of course. Of course she has read a bunch of them, the information avalanche if you start to date someone prominent in a field you're not interested in. Looking him up is like looking up H. G. Wells, or Babe Ruth, or Scarlatti, or the guy who played the brother in that old show everyone loved. She's found out all sorts of stories.

"Now you tell me something," the Vic says.

"I've heard that story before."

"What?"

"The dog story. But it wasn't quite the same. When I read it, you were on the beach, not in the Grove."

"They got it wrong."

"Or you told it wrong, I bet."

"Padgett."

"You *did*." Her astonishment restabilizes her a little, like a bolt of something strong. "I was going to tell you a high school thing, something *real*, and you tell me this dog *bullshit*."

"It's not bullshit."

"It is total bullshit."

"No."

"Did it happen at the beach or in the woods?"

"The woods." The Vic takes a curve, high over the spray of the Pacific. "They were taking a picture of me. And the picture was on the beach. So I just said that it happened on the beach, but the story is true."

Padgett shoves him, slaphappy. "You changed it. The poor dog."

"You're sharp," the Vic says, "spotting that."

She lazes a foot up onto the expensive dashboard, just to watch him check his frown. "Meaning what?"

"Meaning, I like you. I really do, Padgett. We could be, together, very good. I keep trying to say it, but—"

"—but I keep only half-believing you. Why? Why do you take me with you?"

"I can be vulnerable with you," he says, staring straight out the windshield.

"You were trying to con me," Padgett tells him.

"What?"

"That story."

"No. I altered the truth of a story, OK, but that was just for the publicity."

"That's the same thing. What did your wife think when you pulled stuff like that?"

The Vic's face tenses up and then shrugs down. "It was Maureen's idea, actually. But you tell me something now."

"Some bullshit story? OK. I wrote this song."

They listen to it for a minute, some dude saying she's the hottest girl to ever slide into the club. "About my mother," Padgett finishes.

"OK, stop. I'll tell you, OK? This is a no-bullshit thing I am not showing anyone. First, let's grab a lunch. It's right nearby and they have this great sandwich."

"Who are you?" she asks him.

The car pulls up to a raggedy parking lot full of shirtless guys and jeeps. He puts on different sunglasses.

"Master of disguise," she says.

"You can wait in the car. What do you want on your sandwich? They have one really great one."

"Don't get me that. Get me a sad soggy terrible sandwich, thanks."

He checks his wallet and waves good-bye. Padgett loses herself for a moment among the attractive young men out the window, and has the usual daydream, whenever a boy leaves a girl in a car, of tearing out of there. But then the Vic is bounding back with two paper sacks and a bottle of beer, tall like a church spire in his fit hand, with a complicated mess of cork and strap for a top.

"Drink up."

"It's eleven something in the morning."

"Don't bullshit a bullshitter. You snuck the wine from the lobby before we left, didn't you?"

The label cold-sweats in her hand. A drawing of a monk, the words *chocolate* and *hops*. "Are we going to eat in the parking lot?"

"We'll eat after."

The sacks hit the backseat, where an empty plastic throne waits for the baby who, Padgett realizes, must have been in someone's care all weekend. The bottle comes open like a belt buckle and she drinks, prickly with thirst and questions. It's strong, muggy, the first taste. Not her liking, usually. "What are we doing?"

"Do you want to see something? About ten miles more. I'll show you this, something real from me, no disguise or polish. Now polish it off."

She swigs again, and the beer moves around in her stomach like a hungry shark. Her heartbeat is undisguised in her ears. It feels so strong. "Every mogul has one," he is saying, "but mine's a secret."

"Did you just say *mogul*? Did you just call yourself—"

"Tycoon," the Vic says, chuckling. "Bigwig. Fat cat. Titan of industry. One guy's making a train, the other one's fixing Africa. There's guys building a big clock in the desert, have you heard this? Lasts for a thousand years. Nine generations hence they'll thank those clock builders."

"Hence?" she asks. "I'm not sure in the deep future they'll really be thanking them for a clock. They won't need a clock."

"What do you think they need?"

"My guess," Padgett says, still sipping, "is money."

The Vic nods. The music's still going, the thick beer like a sweater on her tongue. She looks back at the empty car seat, and then at the father of the baby, taking a turnoff no one ever takes, down a street where every restaurant, every business, looks worn-out and suspicious. She cannot have another life, but maybe, tilting more of the bottle into her sour mouth with a chain-link alley everywhere out the windows, there's another way to live. City Hall has boosted the audio on the buses designed for the visually impaired, and Padgett hears it all over town: *Doors are opening.* The

Vic might take her someplace—this is in fact what he is
already doing—someplace less pointless and helpless than,
every day, where she lives now. Look at them, in the sideview
mirror if you tilt it right. They're a couple. They're heading
somewhere. Boy would her mother love it, another transfu-
sion of money into the family, no need to liquidate the Bottle
name, the Padgett home. Would *she* love it? His eyes in the
sunglasses are cavernous, something a bear might sleep in.
And the bear, she guesses, is her.

They stop.

"Here?" Padgett asks. "What's here?"

"You couldn't trace this back to me with an army of actu-
aries. Drink up. Liquid courage."

Liquid never feels courageous to Padgett. It's too easily
procured. The bottle's almost done and she's not braver, just
more at odds. The Vic has opened a gate in a fence, the sort
of gate that looks permanently locked, rusty forever in a field
of blank cement and barbed wire. The buildings, windowless
and warehousy, stretch up way over Padgett's buzzy head. She
has no idea where they are, any of these buildings, or the man,
famous and sunglassed, who is punching into a pad of
numbered buttons to make a steel door slide badly up, or her.
Why did Martin let her go, the night of the party, up the
spiral stairs and home with this *mogul*? The barman has not
answered anything or showed up on her screen. She misses
him drying glasses at the bar and hunching over his list, the
one for the party reading

limes
cheap ginger ale for extras

music setup
Shandra at Hallowed

and did it really say

Padgett + The Vic

with a box around it and an arrow, or is that something she dreamed up? Is this a plan? Inside it is dark, and this wealthy man is beckoning. A plan so twisty, a scheme so thorny it must be made of pricks.

"Come on in."

"Vic, what is this?" She can hear herself slurring.

"Something we're working on," he says, and switches on lights. There's nothing in the very large room, just a clean desk and two chairs and someone's can of soda. The Vic walks to it and tips it into a very cheap office trash bin where it gongs loudly. It hardly looks like a business, whatever it is. It looks like a front. In the corner, when her eyes adjust, is a tarp, bright blue and too new. The mogul tugs it into his arms and Padgett can see there's a large hole in the floor, dark inside and rough around the edges like they made it themselves. He beckons again.

"Seriously?"

"This is serious," he tells her. There's a narrow ladder, the rungs too close together so it's more like train tracks, leading straight down.

"You are freaking me out."

"Bwa ha ha," the Vic deadpans. "I'm trying to show you something. Nobody has seen this."

"Maureen?"

"*Definitely*, especially not her *ever*. Come on. It's light down there."

She peers down and sees that the ladder ends in a room, maybe fifteen feet down, where there is the glare and hum of fluorescent lighting. "You got me drunk to go down a ladder?"

"You got yourself drunk."

"Look at me."

He does, he looks at her. He looks fine, just a guy, casually dressed next to a big hole. She puts her hand on his. "I don't know what this is."

"Nobody does," he says, and starts down. On the ladder he looks vulnerable, which he said was the point. She basically has to go down after him. The metal of the ladder is warmer than it looks, almost hot in her hot hands. There's a smell, and halfway down the ladder she traces it to another garbage can, this one large and outdoorsy. The smell is cheap food, garlic and grease, Chinese takeout maybe. And when the Vic helps her down the last rungs, the garbage can is the only thing in the room. No. There is a large metal cage in the corner, the size of a small car, rectangular and empty, something that makes Padgett think of one long-ago scary day at the circus.

"This could be big," the Vic says. He is smiling like a boy with a joystick, and then Padgett sees that the cage is not empty at all. The occupant moves out of the shadows of the room and she feels her skin crawl away from it.

The story is this: When the Vic, not yet known or famed or moneyed, first made his way to California in a van crammed with all the things he owned—*and a dream*, it says in the magazine article—he stopped at a youth hostel somewhere in blazing Arizona and ended up adopting a dog, mangy and boundlessly jazzed up, a mix of every large wild breed, left tied to a bike rack with a thick rope that prickled his fingers when he untied the knot. Finally in San Francisco, before even going to crash with his buddy (now a major shareholder), he took a celebratory walk in a little forest—not the beach—so the dog could shit and bolt around and he, soon to take tech by storm, could just breathe. Another owner was there, with a dog of the small yippy throw-pillow variety. The dogs went at each other, surprising everyone. By the time Vic yelled his way over, the big dog had the small dog in his jaws. Vic, uncharacteristically, did not know what to do, but the other owner, frantic but sure-footed, had a knife in her pocket, and the Vic left the forest without a dog.

The Vic told this story a lot, nudging it, shifting it, detailing and disguising each little move. He conned it out, the way he conned the deal out of Cogwheels, the money out of the music, tycoon, titan, widow, father. He made it work. He moved forward. These men, Padgett thinks, as the cage rattles. These men and their plans.

CHAPTER 3

THE DROUGHT LETS up at cocktail hour. The first rain in months comes down while the town's still badly lit and dim outside Bottle Grove. Inside the bar it's cozy, with some new hip lightbulbs in the fixture, orangish and flickery, almost approximating candlelight, and there are new drinks, samples on the counter in an optimistic summery vein. The citrus and sugar has made it jolly among the few drinkers, so Martin and Stanford are kept busy not just mixing drinks but replying, clarifying, right-you-are-ing and settling disagreements via the jukebox. It's playing Pérez Prado, sprightly King of the Mambo, and the elephant whinnies of the trumpets, the rain's patter-patter, the bitching about real estate and shaky portfolios, for a long while bury the sounds outside until they are unignorable. They are the sounds of a woman screaming.

Martin wipes his hands and goes out, the towel going limp in the weather. The well-dressed woman is in a screaming heap in a scummy planter on the sidewalk, a broken square growing soil and a wan tree and spat-out gum and trash, and she does not fit in it. Her slender feet, her stylish ruined shoes, kick at the rain and the ground, and there's a newspaper over

her head, melted down to a shroud of shelter. In the rain it's
a bad day to be a newspaper, as if they haven't suffered enough
already. At Martin's footsteps she shakes and shudders and
the screams, now, are savage and ravaging.

"Take it easy," Martin says. He throws the towel down and
displays both empty hands, but the woman's hunched over,
face covered, so you can't tell who she is.

"I *saw it*," or something, is what she is screaming.

"Easy."

But it doesn't look easy. The tree branches let go of some
measure of water, right on the newspaper, and the woman
startles with a raw, yowling sound. The newspaper gives
up and Martin watches her grab at the pieces with little
batty hands. You can go mad anywhere, he thinks. Earth
is your bonkers canvas, but it's here that you're doing it, wet
desperate lady. "I *saw*," she says, and curls over a bit. The
scraps of newspaper, torn and soaked, parade down her top.
Her buttons are big and clattery as she moves, still sprawled
in the planter.

"Take my hand."

Her head rolls to face him, and then back again. Martin
gets only a glimpse of her crazy-wretched eyes. "I saw it," she
says. "Something ran at me. It charged me. It did this at my
arm." She rolls up her sleeve but her skin just looks rained on.
No, maybe there's a scratch. He reaches out a hand and she
screams again, draws back like a damsel in an old movie.

"*Hey*," the barman says. She is moving with all limbs
puppety, a large wet purse adding more complication, her
head down so her hair looks like a smeary face. Her pose
makes Martin think of the thirsty, ragged men in cartoon

deserts, rasping *water, water.* He steps toward her again and from under her hair she, yikes, bares her teeth.

"OK, *enough,*" Martin says. "Get it together. Snap out of whatever this is."

She wails, a softer sound but no less spooking.

"I mean it," Martin says. If he doesn't pick up the towel now he will forget, so he does. His necktie is distastefully wet and tired. "Times like this, that shit is catching. Come in and we'll call somebody you need, warm up."

She has crawled, backward, out of the muddy planter, and now crouches slowly into standing, like the chart of evolution.

"Come on."

"Don't let her in here," says one of two guys in the doorway. New customers, a nice article onscreen this week has brought in a spate of this type. They look like what they drink: strong, carelessly made whiskey in short stout glasses for too much money. It's a boon, Martin has to tell himself, the money they bring in even as their boasts and jokes muck up the vibe.

"Not your call," Martin says to them. "You don't get a vote. This is America."

But the guy, with rummy bravado, blockades a little. His friend just shakes his head and continues to wear suspenders. The woman's eyes bulge and swivel like a freaked horse.

"Move," Martin says, "out—"

"You saw her. Shit, we *all* heard her. She's a maniac."

"Everyone in the whole world is a maniac. Get out of my way."

"OK, but this woman is total bananapants. You don't want mentally, what's the word?"

"Disturbed," Suspenders offers.

"*People*," the first guy finishes.

Martin stands up straight. "This is not a talk we're having. There was no call to conversation. Get out of the doorway of my goddamn bar."

The two men keep staring but they step open like doors on their last legs. The barman herds her on through. The woman is so wet and muddy it's like a buffalo roaming in. The bar gets surprised and then adjusts as she leans, wheezing, toward the liquor.

Stanford gives her a towel but he's looking at Martin. "What happened?"

"Give her a hot toddy."

He nods, turns to work.

"*Now.*" Martin barks it.

"The water," Stanford says patiently. "If I do it *now*, it's a warm toddy."

Martin tosses the towel where it goes, and then points at the men frowning from the entrance. "And those two gentlemen are nixed and done. Bill them and show them the door."

"*What?*" Suspenders says.

Martin is already removing their half-finisheds. "What I said."

"You're throwing us out for offering advice?"

"I have the conch. We're not arguing or continuing to argue."

"That's like a First Amendment thing."

"Don't get fucking constitutional," Stanford says, and the woman blows her nose on a paper napkin, but even as a shivery pile, there's something about her that indicates privilege and money. Perhaps it is the lumpy purse, which she plops onto the bar sideways accidentally, and a thick roll of bills tumbles out like a gangster prop. The First Amendment fan puts his wallet on the bar and says to Suspenders, "I told you. I told you this place was too *faggot fancy.*"

These last two words are spat at Martin, but the wallet's already in Stanford's large hands being rifled through. "First of all, boys, *I'm* the faggot," he says. "In fact, Faggot Fancy was my nickname in high school. And now you're banned for life. This cash here is your very generous and mortified tip for your shitty behavior, and good night."

He tosses back the empty wallet to the man who does not catch it, being drunk, but must scramble for it and a few of its flown items, losing forever a hole-punched coupon for coffee drinks. But Martin is looking at the woman and her fading plight. She has reset herself a bit and is waiting, too much cash in hand, for her drink, and is drying her face with another towel. Martin looks at the soggy bills, the president's face also damp and unfamiliar. Who's on the hundred, is what he is wondering, but he just says, "Are you OK?"

The woman can't seem to answer yet. The banned men have tramped outside through the rainy doorway where another woman is standing. It is Padgett, remembering what she loves about Martin Icke.

She's arrived late, having plotted to show up at five. Too much time bided at a worse, grainier bar. Her mouth has bourbon all over the place.

"Martin."

She and Stanford say it at the exact same time. They both want him to look at her. He already has, though, and boardinghouse-reaches across the bar for two glasses, tinkling together in one hand, and a bottle with an emblazoned label. He heads over to the little bench by the jukebox, which has tired of mambo and is playing an angry something about youth. He smiles when he sits down, and Padgett trails along to him with a wave to Stanford and one finger lollygagging down the length of the bar, swerving into space to avoid the woman whose toddy has arrived, and a couple, self-conscious, who have tried the summer samples and are drunker than planned.

There's not really room for two on the bench, which is part of its trick. You practically have to make out if you're sitting together.

"Thanks for coming," he says, his voice shaky.

Padgett nods and narrows herself into the bench. Martin pours them both something and then puts the bottle in front of the jukebox like it's looking the songs over. The muddy woman wanders to one of the tables, and Martin looks over at her but stops looking after her. There's hospitality, he believes in it, and then there's Padgett here in front of him.

"I like this," she says, after the first sip.

"It's a new rum from the Anderson Valley," he small-talks. "They age it in a whiskey barrel."

"That's how *I'm* aging," Padgett says. "Are the glasses new, too? They feel new."

"The new customers love them, their dads drank from this kind of thing, or so they picture it. Local guy, old Italian method." Martin tilts the glass to show off the cut. Padgett tilts hers too and spills rum on her shoe.

"Whoops. I'm an idiot."

"No," Martin says. "You're very smart."

She kisses him. She basically has to. With the drinks, they each only have one hand free and she keeps one on his knee and he on her hair, then her breast. Then they stop. And her breath, is another thing he has missed, of which he neglected to take note in his late-night catalogs. "OK, *that* was probably not smart," he allows.

There's a little laughter in the room, from three drinkers together, not at them. *My friends stay up way too late* is the lyric of the song. *You can't have love if you don't have hate*, although it's not clear if these two things are part of the same thought. Padgett thinks about the Vic, her mogul, and the closet he cleared, too wide and wondrous for the meager things she brought over. Of course, she thinks with a long sip, it was probably Maureen's closet. Next to her is Martin, his tie all rack and ruin like a hangman's ghost. Both fond of her. Perhaps she is the low sort who will go home with anyone. The drink connects these two last thoughts like the word *and*.

"So, um," she says.

"I'll get to it in a minute. Meantime, how about how was your day?"

"I woke up and had tea and toast and a Bloody Mary while he went jogging—"

"The Vic. You can say his name."

"I can say *anyone's* name," she says, "but *yes*, and you know his name."

"I hear you two are getting pretty serious."

"*Seriously?*"

"No, *serious*. You two are getting pretty *seriously* doesn't make sense."

"I mean *seriously*, you—"

Martin grunts in annoyance and takes out his device, poking and sliding at its little screen until there's something to show her. If it were paper, it'd look pawed over. The Vic, saddled up with the baby, on a sidewalk looking distracted and happy. Padgett is two steps behind. "'The Vic appears to be rebounding quicker than VicSpec's stock,'" the barman reads. "'Two recent parties had the mogul—'"

"If it makes you feel better I don't really *remember* those parties," Padgett says, "and don't say *mogul*."

"I'm not saying *mogul*. *They* are, and they're saying *girlfriend*."

"You have not called me or otherwise tugged me on the sleeve," Padgett says, "since—"

"Since you went gold-digging with a man worth—"

She slaps him, hard. She's had practice, from watching old movies and fighting with old boyfriends. The couple shut up so they can gasp and gape, the most interesting time they've had in a bar since who knows. Martin takes it, and, a full twenty seconds later, silent except for verse three of the song, uncorks the bottle for a refill and hands it to her deadpan. She forgets or abandons her fancy glass and swigs it straight, and for a second it looks to everyone, everyone in the world engaged in this, like she's going to spit it in his face. But instead she swallows it down, then hands back the bottle and puts the glass on the ground and says, "I saw your list."

"My—?"

"*Padgett + The Vic*, don't say you didn't write it. You hand-picked it and set it up. You told me you had plans. That's what they were. So don't start with *gold-digging*."

"I was just *bartending*," Martin says, but he is quiet with it, and Padgett knows at this sinking time that she is right. It was a real list and she really saw it.

They're quiet for the song's bridge, a fragile one.

"I have a lot of plans," Martin says finally, "but not one that has ever spun out the way I thought it up." He drinks too, from the same bottle, both glasses forgotten along with the other left-behind trash to pick up at closing. "My life," he says, "what is the word, I just lost it, that they call musicals nobody likes? A *flop*, so far. Stanford and I are drowning up to our eyeballs."

"You're depressed."

"Well, we're in a depression. I mean, we pick up customers here and there, and the rent's not due here and there, you know?"

"Maybe if you didn't throw them out."

"That's one plan. But I thought, you know, of another. And I was right. The Vic, you should have seen when he saw you, went right for you and you kept him laughing. Right? Teams of money men can't get him to sit still for thirty seconds, and you guys talked for almost *two hours* before he drove you home."

"Except it wasn't home. You set me up. I'm bait."

"Padgett, I will beg if necessary."

"Why don't you tell me just what the plan was."

"*Is*. I just thought, you're a coaxy gal. He's a titan of industry."

"Stop."

"Look, it is just a matter of moving some money, which he is rolling in, to the pocket of somebody else who cannot at present rub together two dimes to make a fire."

"So you propose—"

"Well, *he's* not going to propose, is he? He's a grieving widower. But there's money. You know there is. I thought, you pal around with him, the money kind of slides my way."

"So, for the money?"

Martin looks around the bar like something has scurried into the place. "What did you think."

"You just want—? Why would you do this for the money?"

"*That*," Martin says, "is a question only rich people ask. Because I don't have any. We can't all just crash in Mommy's little mansion."

Padgett clenches her hands so she will not say, *You know this?*

"I did my research after the ninth time you changed the subject," Martin tells her. "Your family owns fucking *Bottle Grove.*"

"She's on the *board.*"

"It's the same thing."

"I'm sorry she was a bitch at the wedding, but that is not *remotely*, on the largest *map*, anywhere *near* the same thing as owning—"

"Close enough," Martin says, gesturing around the half-empty business.

"No," Padgett says, "enough's enough. Yes. I'm *those* Bottles. From *those* Padgetts. You can pedigree me up to the first people to fuck up this whole area, probably. But I have nothing to offer. I'm locked out of the money. That's how they do it, rich people, if you must know. I get a little bit every month, just enough for not doing anything, really. So there's nothing I can do in my whole goddamn life."

At this, Martin can't help rolling his eyes. "You could get a *job*."

"I don't," Padgett says, "want a job."

He can't roll his eyes twice in ten seconds, and besides, he can admit that yes, she has a point. "Look," he says, "I got lucky a little, a little while back. From *nowhere*, from a five-star review Stanford's ex-*boyfriend* wrote and posted, they call me up about the speakeasy. Do you know what we charged them, the Vic and his new venture vultures, to hang out with call girls until he deigns to show up for a five-minute pep speech?"

"Call girls, I *knew* it."

"I just thought you could land him. You *could*."

Padgett grabs at the bottle. "I'm not a goddamn call girl."

Martin swigs and hands it over. "I *know*! That's why it could work."

"Let me think," she says, and takes her sip. "Well."

"Well?"

"There's a safe."

"What?"

"It's behind this still life he has on the wall in his study. He thinks I don't know. One day we were drinking brandy in there and, he won't remember, he took a key out of this big jeweled book, large like a Bible but hollow inside. You know the kind. And when he was asleep, I crept so quiet to find the key and slip the painting down from the wall. And when I got it open—I'm upset the way you're looking at me, that you sort of believe all this."

Martin's flush looks flushier in the jukebox lights. "I do not," he says.

"We're not in the golden age of caper heists."

"I know what we're in."

"Money isn't like that now, if it ever was, a pile of rubies or gold from a galleon. We aren't pirates. This money is foxed away, it's pretend money, it's the idea of money, the profit made from betting that some other pile of money wouldn't get doubled from betting on some other pile. You want a lamp? He has a lamp we could resell someplace for a month's rent, if you're ready to have the getaway car idling outside with a big trunk in back for stolen lamps."

"I do not want a lamp." His hands are sloppy on the bottle and she looks and sees his eyes shimmering, as if in reply to the jukebox. He's crying? Or, yes, the room has just collapsed a little; it often does at this time of drink.

"What *do* you want," she says, quietly, not really asking a question, and puts a hand on the back of his neck. Martin leans in so her arm is tricked around him and she watches him smile at the luck and the pressure of it.

"A parade."

My friends stay up way too late.

"What?"

"I don't," he says, miserably, "have the education for the moneygrubbing, but my dad used to water down bourbon and let me watch them play poker, a bunch of old men talking."

"Your dad was a gambler? Professionally?"

"He never did *anything* professionally. So I'm trying to figure it out, Padgett." His arm takes a slow sweep around the bar. "The only recognition I need is for someone to signal for a refill. But if I don't learn the know-how to get better at this, I'll get tossed to Portland, Oregon."

"Heaven forbid," Padgett says.

"Well, I see you don't live there either. In this city everyone's scheming for a monument, I get that, and I've got to latch on to some location, some tiny little plot I can hatch while they skyscraper up everything. I picture it like a parade, you know? Just a little happy march in my honor. Flowers tumbling down from the windows. Piñatas, kids with confetti, dogs barking in the streets, a parade is my vision, and don't look at me like it's ridiculous stupid because I know it is."

He leans back into her arm. It is, she thinks, ridiculous and stupid, she's in agreement about that. To wait for a parade, to be putting your own clothes in a dead wife's closet, to be photographed leaving a party, making glasses the old Italian way, to be married—and here she is thinking of the night they met—in a fake forest. Ridiculous dreams in a sack, and then you share a sack with some other ridiculous dreamer. They are kissing again and finishing the bottle. "I'll help you," she says. "I'll get it for you."

"No you won't."

"I will, I will." She has been looking, it's true, for the reason she's staying with the Vic. This is it. Another man is not the best reason, maybe, but if not a job—

"Why would you?"

"It's right, you're right." She's hungry at his mouth. "He's a schemer, he's unscrupulous. He lives like you wouldn't believe. I don't believe it. It scares me, what he's got socked away . . ." She trails off here, looks fruitlessly for her reflection in the jukebox window. "Or locked in a basement."

Martin turns the done bottle like a wheel in his hands. "If you married him," he says, "both of us could get what we want, I think."

"He's not going to marry me," Padgett says, and sighs like a math teacher giving up on the slow kid. "I am barely grasping the banister of my life, and he is crowning himself king of his own goddamn accomplishments. His dead wife was a *mover*, another powerful icon or what have you. Some school based on the principles of Japanese folklore."

"Yeah, I think I clicked on that somewhere."

"With cabernet in him, he won't stop talking about it. He has a *baby*, and the very thought of children *panics* me, that they *exist*."

"Don't pretend he's icky to you."

"*You're* icky, Icke."

"You know what I'm asking," he says, nervous and rough in his throat. "Do you want him? Or do you want—"

"Sometimes," she says, the bar getting spinnier. "Don't growl like that. I'm just telling you the truth. The water pressure in his shower is the most—"

"Well, it's the truth too that I'm jealous. He takes off your clothes. That's the worst part. I close up here, and go home and think about him slipping you out of your underwear."

"Don't think like that, then. And *you* handed me over. Pal around, you just said it."

"It was just a plan then."

She stands up and there it is, plain in front of her, the two of them and how desperate they are. It's a privileged and lofty peninsula here, where they gad about town. But that craft out on the horizon, bobbing happy and calm—that's the boat they missed. Catch it, she thinks fiercely. Catch it now. "It's a plan now. Isn't it?"

"It is," the barman agrees, and in this way they are troth. She heads gracelessly out of the bar, into a night all speckly with the rain over. It's her turn to almost cry, and crying she beckons an onscreen car. The driver seems to get it, and turns down music on a system that, she notices blurrily, belongs to the man she's calling.

"Hi."

"It's Padgett."

"I know, Padgett. How did it go?"

She told him the truth, about Martin and where she was going. It seemed like the easiest way to cover it up. "It was upsetting, actually," she says.

"Did you let him down easy?"

"Well, it wasn't easy to let him down."

"What did you tell him?"

"How do I know? Half the time I wasn't listening."

"You sound drunk."

"Well," she says, looking through the window. The raindrops' mosaic spatters constellations on the wild nothing off the side of the road. "That's due, I would say, to drunkenness."

The Vic sighs into her ear, through a phone he gifted and set up for her. She's undoubtedly a dot on his screen, tagged and moving, another reason not to lie to him. "I wish you would do less of that."

"Yes," she says, nodding slowly, largely, watching the moon keeping pace with her eyes.

"I'm getting serious about you."

There is no single thing in the world she can think to say.

"I want you to get serious about me too."

Her situation, she thinks, has not improved, in terms of knowing how to reply to him.

"I'm glad you're not seeing him anymore. I mean, who is he, anyway, besides a cocktail slinger?"

"He's a schemer," she says, with difficulty.

"Good riddance, then."

"OK."

She hears the rustly wait through the phone, the loud pauses of our times. He probably hears the wheels spinning her through puddles.

"What are you thinking?" he says finally.

Time for the truth again. "That I look ugly when I cry."

"Then I guess I'd better keep you happy. Stay up, OK? Stay up at home for me. Stop drinking, there's restoration water and a baguette."

"OK."

"Don't sneak the Polish vodka anymore."

"OK."

"That is literally a twelve-hundred-dollar bottle."

But you got it for free, Padgett suspects, but, "OK."

"See you later, then."

"OK."

"I love you," he says, for the first time.

"OK," she says. It is jumpy, when something goes exactly according to plan. They will be, they *are* latched together, she and this titan of industry, another quick deal in this town, in it for the money, and good for business, she knows, for a glossy newcomer to have on his arm a local girl from a good, Padgett guesses is the word, family. Not to say they aren't excited for each other anyway. She wants him. The car carries her, still crying, up, up, to where he lives, high above most low places, like debt-teetering bars. Martin, outside, is cold and his arms are uncomfortable. He forgot to hold his shirt cuffs when he put on his sweater, something he learned when he was a little boy. He breathes for a minute before his phone chimes in. All the smoky rum suggests that it has been a good day, although it hasn't. So he picks up without looking.

"Hello?"

"Tell me what you see in her."

He looks back at the bar. "Give me a break, Stanford."

"Because I was looking at this coffee-table book about train wrecks—"

"*Stop.*"

"Bay Area Rapid Transit already took your shoe. Is it going to rip up your sleeve, which in your case, has your heart—"

"Don't make me come in there."

"Here where you work? Perish the thought. That girl, Martin, is going straight downhill."

"Even downhill has an uphill side," Martin says hopefully. "Look, I've never dated a crazy person before."

"That's true," Stanford says, with a short laugh and an "Any particular vodka?" to someone inside asking for a Greyhound. "You usually ruin women. This woman will ruin herself. This is not a step up."

"If something awful was going to happen to her," Martin says, "it would have happened already."

"How did you reach that conclusion?"

"Like everybody does, by totally believing it. Look, my bulbs have burned out a little lately. She's flash. You know? An open door on a quiet block."

"You know you're describing our bar."

Martin hangs up and walks in.

"Martin!" Stanford says, like a long-lost something. He has coffee for him, hands it over. "Do me a favor and sober up. It's too early for you to be this sloppy."

Martin sips and frowns and joins Stanford behind the bar. "This is all easy for you to say. Gay men can cat around all the time. The most hideous homo in the world can have a sex life gorgeous straight men can only dream of." He sips and grimaces into the cup.

Stanford's eyes blink once. "I bet, if you put your mind to it, you could think of some drawback in the life of a gay black man."

"OK, yes, sorry, but support your comrade in his romantic journey. She has money. Plus, she's crazy about me."

"You're half right, dude."

Martin gives up and smiles and roams the place tucking away empties and bringing them back like a stumbly honeybee. Bottle Grove is filling up, a few packs of entitled people to whose money he and Stanford are entitled. It won't be a bad night, moneywise, although he'd feel better if more people were ordering artisanal and complicated, instead of a lot of beer bottles with the labels peeled off as they talk, like eucalyptus bark. The men nursing them are smiley and should either shave or hole up for awhile until the beards work.

"Can I get this out of the way?" the barman says to them.

"This and *this*," says the beardier one. "It was on the floor. Looks important to somebody. What's a Padgett?"

Inscrutable to one, crucial to another, like every other scrap in life. It's an old list of Martin's. He can see Padgett's name right above *Gin*, so many substances he's too into. He crumples it into his pocket, and tells them thanks and nudges them into two doubles of a whiskey Martin identifies as good for sipping after beer. It's not a lie. Like a mime, he points to Stanford and points to the bottle and points to two glasses, twice, and Stanford nods like, that's more like it.

Martin slides into a chair opposite the woman who started the night screaming. She's mostly restored now, restroomed clean with an empty toddy glass in front of her. She stares at him seated and takes a hopeful last sip that's not more than three drops. She keeps staring until he puts his coffee cup down and then she keeps staring.

"I thought you asked if you could ask me a question," she says, each word drifting in space.

He shakes his head. "Just making sure. You were rough out there when you came in."

"You helped me," she says, and moves the wet bangs from her eyes a little until he recognizes her, it took a while without the movie star getup, as the woman screaming at the vicar, the forest, the fight, the car crash. "Thank you."

"You're from the wedding. What happened?"

She blinks. "Reynard."

"I didn't mean—"

"I don't remember your name."

"Martin."

"Nina."

"OK, right. So, tonight."

"Tonight?"

"Screaming."

She reaches a little and in one shaky flourish drinks the rest of his coffee, smacking her lips like a kid. "I was mugged."

"Mugged."

"Don't call the police."

"I assure you they haven't been called. But, if you've been mugged."

"It's not something I want to describe to authorities."

Drunker, he decides, than one hot toddy, although his own judgment is full of rum. He just points to a ripple at her feet, like a loyal cat, an anchor of wet weight. "Good thing they didn't take your purse, those muggers."

Nina's legs encircle it, hug it to the table leg. "I ran from it."

"It."

"The muggers. I guess I yelled and they gave up."

There's something about her eyes, relined since the incident, that taps him a little. He sees this frequently as a barman. She wants to tell him something. She pulls at her top, drags it around her like the room's drafty. "Why don't you say what happened," he tries.

"I *said* what happened," she says, getting sharp. She puts down the drink like the drink thinks so, too. "I was mugged, and thanks for taking me in, but I don't need to be subjected."

"Wait," the guy says, with his new whiskey. "Did you say you were mugged? I couldn't help hearing."

"Tonight," Nina says. "Almost broad daylight."

"That's so *weird*," he says. "I was mugged three nights ago two blocks away."

"I was mugged last year in Golden Gate Park," says a woman whose boyfriend is in the bathroom. She has a dash of salt on the bridge of her nose, from the rim of a margarita glass, and nighty night, Martin stands up, knowing the avalanche has arrived. In bars such stories get told in a pileup, burying whatever else the drinks might otherwise have revealed. Martin grabs the toddy glass and skedaddles to Stanford's side. Stanford is squeezing a lime into a tonic like he's boarding up windows. They don't even have to meet eyes.

"*I* was mugged in the park," says somebody else. "Years ago after a show I was taking a shortcut on foot. Two kids I swear looked twelve pushed me down into the gravel and then held my head down like I was eating it. I thought I would die but my wallet was gone."

"A guy in an Afro, nothing personal, flagged me down at like eleven thirty on Union. He had a bill in his hand saying *Can you change me?* When I took out my wallet he just *pounded* my hand against the brick and I let go and he was gone and now, everyone says I'm racist, but I wouldn't take out my wallet if the Pope needed a five."

"They do that, the distraction. In Guatemala my girlfriends and I, for a bachelorette thing, and the concierge ends up telling us they work with the *street musicians*, if you can believe it. Classic con. The percussionist so *loud* and when people are listening they cut into our purses with a *razor*. Holding a bag beneath—"

"Anything flashy. Bourbon Street, six million people around, this old man of fucking seventy-five if he was a day, and pardon my language. Seersucker. I remember he says, asking me after getting his cigar lit, if I was *ever lucky enough to be on an airplane at sunset*. It sounded so fascinating—"

"A man, filthy so I should have known—"

"Oh, *I* should have known. I mean, who wouldn't have known?"

"This lawyer I know was in Milan by himself, ends up drinking alone next to another American. *Hey, let's try this bar I heard about.* They hold his card for the bill, and at the urinal there's a knife to his throat."

"Scuttle in the bushes, and I can't help turning around. My high school ring."

"Cash I made six months tipping, I always figure someone at the restaurant tipped somebody off. The proverbial alley. I had to tell my girlfriend there were no tickets. There was crying."

"Can you say *transvestite* or is it all *gender* now? Someone with a beard and a dress, I am saying, with the oldest rustiest gun you ever—like a cowboy movie, but who takes chances?"

"The police said, well, it helps with statistics."

"They said check lost and found, and I thought, the only thing you're going to find in lost and found are idiots checking lost and found. They said *no* and I said *si* and they went in back and there in a bag was my camera."

"Tacked up was a photo of it. *Found: Executive Briefcase, no questions asked.* Can you believe it? *Found, no questions asked.*"

"Can you believe it? I thought they were going to murder me, minimum."

It goes on the whole hour, the only parade Martin gets tonight or maybe, he looks at the door like she might come back, the rest of his life. "These people," Stanford says to him, both of them thinking of Padgett, "are. Trying. To. Kill. Us."

CHAPTER 4

I s the milk warm enough?"

"Yes, Vic."

"You sure?"

Padgett is looking at a drop of milk on her wrist, a small albino island uncharted and uninhabited. Never in her life did she think she would approach a place like this. When her brother was born, pink and stinky, Padgett—four years old and still *Gail* then—had vowed that never would such a thing as a baby be in her life. It has been an easy promise to keep, what with birth control, and not being taken for mother material by anyone who has spent any time with her. Through half a bottle of white wine, she tries to concentrate on the temperature of the drop of milk on her wrist. What *is* the temperature? It feels like a drop of milk.

"Yes, Vic."

"Well, let's start her up."

This is the first time she's been allowed to feed Kitsune, from a bottle of milk she's been taught to warm, and did warm, in a pot of water on the stove, after it arrived overnight from one of the many, many women who, learning of

Maureen's death, offered their milk online to him. Kitsune is in her lap, her little lips trying to draw food from the space between them. Padgett, with the Vic watching, waves down at the baby. Kitsune frowns, and Padgett does not blame her. To whom does a baby need to wave? Acquaintances, people in neighboring boats? Why teach waving to a creature constantly surprised by its own hands? She should go out to the backyard orchard, where a bottle of rye is stashed in a bag in a wheelbarrow, and teach the mute plum trees how to sign their names.

The bottle's in. Kitsune sucks. "There you go," the Vic says, to Padgett, so Padgett passes it along.

"There you go, Kitsune. Liquid lunch."

"*Breakfast*," the Vic says.

"Brunch," Padgett counters. It's ten A.M. and Sunday, and Kitsune has been up since four. Sundays here are particularly domestic, almost marital, the invisible housekeeper and personal assistant and both nannies gone, actually vacated and not just rustles in Padgett's peripheral vision. Kitsune wakes early—if a dainty phrase like that can be applied to a howling banshee in the middle of the goddamn night—and the Vic sits and feeds her on the balcony, usually, lit by one of his little screens and the dawning sky. Then they're both in bed with her, this tiny baby and this very wealthy man, both their scents and gurgly breaths passing over Padgett like shifting currents. It gets too light in the room too quickly—the Vic will soon redo the blackout curtains as a gift for her—so they rise, Kitsune's eyes everywhere wondering where the party is. They put her in a—it's made in Sweden, but it's a *cage*, is what it is—and have a quiet breakfast, the Vic with two or sometimes three devices accepting, like horsebacked servants, his marching orders and changes of plans. Padgett fingers her own screen. She doesn't have much, but it won't do to stare out the window, and now she has more than she used to. A few friends of friends ask her if she wants to consult for their companies, none in Padgett's area of expertise since she has none, the asks so blatantly tilted toward the Vic she can hardly look at them. This morning she wants to finish reading the book everyone is reading, so as to have read it, and then later, a drinks date with another girlfriend of another man rich in tech, or whatever it is Padgett has become. Kitsune closes her eyes and basks in the pleasure of the bottle. Padgett's a wet nurse without milk, an executive assistant with live-in privileges, something that feels virtual, so often does it show up onscreen, that's nevertheless based on something that is, she's pretty sure, real.

Most nights they sup late together, after nibbling at two or three quasi-professional gatherings, from food that appears somehow in pots on the burner, pots they leave halfheartedly soaking in the sink, someone else's problem. The screens flicker like candlelight, and when the Vic takes a call outside, or strides off to check something in his office, Padgett finishes the bottle, whatever bottle it is, and for the most part they are in an agreeable semi-silence just like an actual couple. There's sex but not unduly so, not passionate or trashy enough for her to be the widower's rebound party girl she sure as hell looks like to herself. She's drinking more now, but somehow, in her new bewildering circumstance, this just means *she knows a lot about wine*, and similarly she has risen in the language of digital description, once gossiped about as a *former cater-waiter* and now as someone, spotted and phone-documented spitting a clam dumpling into a napkin—*in the world of food*. But Padgett does not know what world she is in. She hasn't been in her old place, her old *bedroom*, in a long time; last she checked it looked like the room of someone who had gone missing, *kept just the way it was on that day*, clothes flat on the floor like a suicided girl, uncoiled headphones on the carpet listening to nothing. And where's her life now? The Vic still lives like she can't believe, and now she can't believe how much she can't believe. She sleeps beside him in a tightly made bed now. Now, she feeds his little baby.

"She likes you," the Vic says.

"She likes *milk*," Padgett says.

He shakes his head, not necessarily in disagreement. "You're good. You're getting good with her."

"Thank you," she says, and holds Kitsune's head, a larger grapefruit than last time. She's half done, so Padgett takes the bottle and hands it to Vic, who turns it carefully in his hands like he's unloading a gun. She lays a towel and then a baby on her shoulder, pit-patting for burps. She faces the Vic's unshaven smile, his eyes jazzed from financial success and too little sleep.

"I have to go in today."

"I had a feeling." One of his interests was merging, or expanding, or what have you.

"Can I leave you with Kitsune?"

What is, she thinks, the line of how much you can drink with a baby in your care, even one surrounded by soft objects in a cage? The Vic, she's learned, tracks his bottles, so she drinks her own, scattered hither and yon, but not too yon, in

the condo's satellite refrigerators and two duffel bags. "OK,"
she says.

"Unless you have plans."

"You know my plans," she says. "Not until five. Until then
I can make the plan of taking care of this duffel. *Bundle.*
Baby."

"It's a big step."

"I'll step it," she says, and with the burping hand she tousles
his hair a little.

"I'll be back in the afternoon."

"I could cancel with Nina, if you let me know."

"I always let you know," the Vic says, not at all accurately.
"So it's OK?"

"I said it was OK."

He sighs, a little sweatily. He wants to be sold on this, she
can see. He is selling *himself* on it, and yet isn't quite sold. "I
need to know—"

"*Vic,*" she prickles. "I'm going to stay in my sweats, read,
answer these people, call up television to watch. Shows you
don't like. And when Kitsune cries, I'm going to put food in
her diaper and change her mouth. And for lunch I'll have the
rest of the pesto from before."

"And no wine."

"On my honor," Padgett says, "the baby will have two
Manhattans and *that's it.*"

He squints at her. "Maybe I should find—"

"Find no one. I will do it and yes, I am ready."

He's honorable enough, she sees, his gaze already sneaking
to the peg with the sweatshirt sprawled on it, to be nervous
about this. But not honorable enough to cancel whatever cash

flow bicker is due to happen around some well-catered table. "This calls for a new phone," he says brightly.

"Vic, *no*. I just learned how to find the restaurants on my new one."

But he's already in the pocket of the sweatshirt. "This is your new one. Bryan's going to call it *Fiona* when it launches."

"Hi, Fiona," Padgett says dully, and reinserts the baby bottle.

"Give me your old one. Play with it today, tell me what you think."

She takes it, another new device from him. The screen has the three of them, her and the Vic and Kitsune strapped on, on a gray and tiny beach. "OK."

"If you need to buy something, there's—"

"I don't know what babysitters charge nowadays—"

"Har har."

"—but I have money of my own." She has twenty-three dollars in a wallet someplace, and—what's the date?—at the first of the month, a princely sum even by San Francisco standards, rent-free obviously, that nonetheless always peters out. She tips big, or, more accurately, forgets her cash on the counters of bars. Her credit digits are zipped tight into these phones the Vic keeps giving her—the newest rectangles, shined up in cases that look like riot gear—so cash is the only way, probably, that she buys things that the Vic doesn't know about. The spending is harder to sneak than the case of wine, behind the forgotten Italian motorcycle with its dusty, ghosty helmet in the second garage. Eventually everything, everyone, can become ordinary. He pauses in the doorway, a famous person, and blows her a kiss like an ad. It makes her feel famous too. She listens to him unlocking the car with a signal from his phone. Her phone can do that too, at least the last one did, if she had a car. It's not feeling famous in a good way, if there's a good way to feel famous. "Kitsune School makes me feel famous," is in fact the slogan of the Vic's school, chartered or founded under the education umbrella of the pile of companies, the lingering influence of dead Maureen. It's something one of the kids said, the Vic had a few quotes he showed Padgett over gin and tonics (four for her, sort of one for him) and she chose the *famous* one. Later, over dinner with two spectacled tech guys whose partnership was professional or romantic or both, the Vic had referred to her as a consultant.

Kitsune spits up on Padgett's shoulder. Padgett sympathizes but puts Kitsune down anyway, safely on the carpet in the room. What is this room, really? It'd had an exercise bike, a very new model, but it's gone. Silly bookshelves, so modern they're just hyphens on the wall, two tables with sharp corners that will bruise you in a drunken stumble, and doesn't Padgett know it. Two vases from Mexico or wherever, or maybe not vases. She scours the room for a target, a hook to hang her somewhat rage. She's always looking for this around here.

She cannot call Martin. She cannot type to him on the phone, or any phone she finds or the six, she thinks it is, computers in the house. There is only her old computer, shut up in a duffel bag with stopped-up wine and running shorts for camouflage, and surely someday this will be cast away, locked out from the Vic's home network. It is old, a dated and silly-looking clamshell in the mogul's sleek palace. It ruffles the Vic that she uses it to listen to music, rather than his own hyperpersonalized home system, so she points to the lullabies she's put on her screen, tinkly tunes for Kitsune that the system hasn't grabbed yet. This is her reasoning to him. But really her old laptop is the last telegraph office, the only carrier pigeon to Martin Icke.

Martin and Padgett chose an old jazz album, obscure but not hip or beloved, up on an old, dying-out site. All the other places log you in and keep track, selling at you and monitoring your hankerings. Here no one cares. It is like meeting Martin in an old abandoned shack, were any such shacks not now condominiums in San Francisco. They're paranoid; they're careful. They use lots of blank aliases, accounts utterly unsupervised, and communicate in the loopy manic scrawl of online comments to pass even further unnoticed. Their correspondence is permanently up underneath the screen that plays the jazz album, tunes Padgett is so tired of she keeps it on mute.

WAYD

is *What Are You Doing* and is Martin.

> I'm babysitting today SO BORED!

could be anyone, but it is Padgett. Two minutes later, Martin replies,

> We should talk sometime soon k?
>> Fed the baby today,

Padgett types, hoping this is sending the message that things are progressing. But maybe Martin thinks the baby is the Vic, or that it's just a euphemism for drinking more. Padgett finds a swig while waiting for Martin to respond.

Do you still like this record tho?

Hellzya

Kitsune mews a little and it makes more sense: *Pay attention to me.* Padgett holds her. It is warm to hold a baby, no one would deny that, and it is nice, also undeniable, to hold something warm. Like wine in the belly. She looks over at this masked conversation. It's even possible that it is not Martin, that someone else is actually listening to their record and liking it. Or Martin means he's busy, that the bar's business is strong. It's like the rustles out the window, this scratchy communication she has with the barman. It's there, she can hear it, but it's not really clear what anything is meaning, or if it means what it says. The rustling birds in the bush, squirrels in the branches, a large burglar raccoon maybe, all sound a little frightening. But they could be spooked themselves, by some larger creature invoking pain and trouble.

Reynard walks cloaked through the neighborhood. One of his hands is running against everything he walks by—shrubs, trees, a wooden fence with each slat tut-tutting his dirty fingers. The other hand holds a cigarette, just one lonely cancerous star, tobacco an almost unusual sight in San Francisco nowadays. The last true cigarettes are seen with banished boyfriends on rusted-out balconies, or petulant white-collars with defiant plumes in lunch-break parks, small

huddled masses under the awnings of bars like the last gatherings of the faithful. Reynard, of course, is not a man of faith.
He is not a vicar or a husband or even a fiancé. He is the
possession of the ghost of a fox. You see such types around
the edges of packs of young men, showered and clapping
shoulders in loud bars, the one whose eyes will gyre silent
around the room while everyone else roars at jokes—in other
words, the one who might rape you. You can track him
onscreen, cold-logic screeding on the topic of the moment.
Observe him underemployed, hunched in a café, crawling
under other customers' legs to plug in his scratchy laptop, how
the legs flee from him.

San Francisco is full of pop-ups and takeovers, French
tourists using someone's two-bedroom apartment for three
days, a sandwich place in the empty chrome shell of the closed
stereo store. This is just another sort. The fox's howling spirit
inhabited him at the moment of impact there in Bottle Grove.
Ferocious and scheming forkedly in a language people do not
speak, it found a space where Reynard's heart was beating
wildly and conned its way in, although it was not as if Reynard
had been previously unconniving or at rest.

Like many impulsive and sudden unions, it was a bad idea.
Still, when he straggled home past dawn, his linen suit torn
and ruined from the inside, one of his upstairs neighbors, the
female half of a quiet happy couple in their twenties, helped
him into his paltry studio and asked what happened, what
kind of wedding could that have been? Within minutes he
was fucking her on the butcher block, and a few days later
when the male half came down to inquire about some nighttime scratchings in the walls, Reynard had him too, and in

the days that followed he spent hours leaving them both terrified and turned on. Like many bitter singles, the phantasm
wants to break up others. Engulfing, or being engulfed with,
this fox ghost has made him more ravenous, and has changed
Reynard's looks considerably. His face flickers, or anyway
changes over, like a mobile in the wind, as unrecognizable as
some of these newly gentrified blocks. In the right light, like
all sneaky fucks he looks like a monster, but then handsome,
as handsome as can be. He crosses town quickly, and a teenage
girl, her moody stares out the window a soundtrack to a
favorite crashy pop album, thinks for a moment some tall and
ferocious animal is there to carry her off in this hateful, smoky
daylight. If only, she thinks, if only, at last. But Reynard's
target is in the bar he's heading toward. I need a drink too,
his ghost says.

Bottle Grove is open. Three people are inside, Martin
Icke puzzling over his phone and half-listening, Rachel
Nickels quite drunk, Stanford Bell downstairs closing up
the speakeasy space, which got busted last night, thanks to
an anonymous tip. Improper fire exits and other violations.
The city is treating the speakeasy as it has speakeasies in
bygone days, shutting them down unless some powerful
patron can bribe away the law. Martin is thinking of this as
he tries to decode Padgett's message under the jazz album, if
it's a message, and if it's Padgett for sure. The Vic could
reopen the speakeasy, help it make a little more money.
Money could help it make a little more money. So could
risking everything by reopening it in secret. Anonymous
tip. Rachel slides ten dollars toward him.

"That for a tip," she says slurrily, "and another."

Martin puts off his device and ambles over. "That's either no drink or a lousy tip."

"For a twenty?"

"It's a ten."

She twists her head to look at it. "I have mistaked so many mades."

"Everybody does."

She switches out the bill. "Is that terrible of me?"

"Is what?"

"What I was saying, about Ben."

Martin shakes ice, covering the sound of not having paid much attention, really. Rachel is increasing her troubled afternoons here, to two per week, usually. Ben has new clients—Martin can't remember what he does exactly, but anyone in San Francisco who can afford a house and a wife who drinks in the afternoons is probably in tech—and she loiters here while he meets late. Honeymoon's over, Martin thinks and pours the drink, raises his coffee to her. They both sip and wince.

"We're thinking," Martin says, "of calling that the New Hat. It's basically a Derby, with the bourbon swapped out for rye, little more Benedictine, little less bitters."

"What was I saying?"

"Your husband."

"I found a schedule laid out on his calendar."

"I don't know what that means."

Rachel's sip is sloppy and she licks her palm after she puts down the glass. "He has a regular calendar, right? And if you type in a code you can see, embedded on top of it, his own personal comments and schedule."

"Why would you do that?"

"I couldn't find him one day."

"And his phone was there?"

"OK, I was snooping. I don't know, I wanted to *know*."

"How did you know his code?"

"It's my birthday. Every code of his is my birthday." She says this and then, perhaps thinking Martin does not believe her, says her birthday out loud, unwisely. Or perhaps she's flirting.

"That's sweet," he says.

Rachel nods so determinedly her chin knocks against her breastbone. "I should be shot, for snooping on such a sweet guy."

"I didn't say that."

"You *thought* it, Martin."

Martin is a little surprised she still remembers his name, through all the rye. "I promise," he says with a little solemnity, "I never thought of shooting you."

"Well," Rachel says, her hands waving for a synonym, "*arrested*, then. Dragged into the station."

"So what was the personal schedule? Hookers?"

"Flowers."

"What?"

"Love notes. You know, no-reason emails. That's what it says, *no-reason emails*. This brand of hot chocolate I like that's Mexican, he buys me that."

"I'm not following you."

She gulps it, this cocktail meant to be sipped, and sipped, Martin thinks, by better clientele. But nobody glam shows. Instead they keep getting these couples in varying states of dissatisfaction. "Me?" she asks.

"You," he tells her. "You are not being followed."

"My husband has a schedule of being nice to me."

"Well, good."

"No, not *good*. I used to think he was *considerate*. But he has technology to help him do it. He doesn't have to think of me. It reminds him to make his wife happy."

"Whoever put that technology together is going to be a rich man."

"Oh, you *know* who put it together," she says, with another slushy sip. "It's like he's pressing buttons."

"Making women happy through something on your phone? One billion, easy."

"There's no *thing* to make women happy. Happiness *is* the thing."

"Well," the barman says, "maybe it's a thing you have to feed once a week with a no-reason email."

She laughs, if you can call it that. "It doesn't have a sex schedule but I already know it, Fridays and Tuesdays plus the weekend if we go out."

She finishes her drink. Martin takes the glass before she breaks it, probably. "OK."

"Best sex I ever had," she says.

"Well, that's good."

"Of course, I had some really terrible sex experiences."

"Well, I'm sorry to hear that. But it's better now, right?"

"I want more of it," she says, but with her purse open and her pointing at the rye so it's clear she means the drink. "I know I'm terrible," she tells him. "I should be condemned. I should be prosecuted. I just get scared of things and they trample all over all the happy things I'm trying to—" her hands tinker in the air "—stack up, I guess I would say, so I can enjoy them."

"Enjoyment is good," Martin says. Her unhappiness is starting to feel jinxy to him, a cloud over his business when business is bad enough.

"It's my own fault. I stomp all over things like a horse with a scary neck."

"I think," Martin says, "that's enough drink for you now, because what are you talking about?"

"I should be dead."

Reynard slips in. They both look up, bride and barman, and for a second remember him and for a second don't. His face alters, narrows and grows hair, fine and wild, his eyes driven and untrustworthy, his fingernails long and filthy and then just normal. The effect is not ghastly, just ghostly, so now he's simply a stranger in the bar who feels, certainly but unprovably, up to no good. Rachel shudders slightly. Reynard sits down on the neighboring stool and disrobes a little. His cloak is just as evil when he takes it off.

"Evening," Martin says.

Reynard looks at his watch—which he beat a man for— and at the door at the fogginess. "Not quite yet."

"It's five o'clock somewhere," Martin says, the standard barman line.

"Indeed," Reynard says, and his eyes slide off to the chalkboard drinks list. He purses his lips at the choices. His teeth move about and Rachel is watching them. She licks her lips.

"Sazerac for me," he says, "and one for the lady if she'll join me."

Martin glances at his shelves, flips an empty bottle. "That drink has Peychaud's in it. I'll need to go down back for a minute."

"That was by design," Reynard not-jokes, and then, his eyelid precise as a guillotine, winks at Rachel. "Wasn't it, deario?"

Deario. Rachel flutters at it, knowing she's being silly, ridiculous. She is married. She married Ben Nickels in a ceremony and everything. This man, of course he is a man despite some animal whisper she keeps half-hearing, smells like cigarettes, something she gave up. When she got tired of lingering outside buildings like a target. He can likely smell the whiskey on her and she has not, shut up she *hasn't*, become a woman who hangs around bars for men to go home with. She just drinks here a little. This morning, every morning, she makes her bed.

"I think this is why there are jukeboxes," Reynard says, "so these awful silences will instead be full of music and joy."

"I'm sorry," Rachel says right away. "I was staring, I think." She still is. Reynard slithers to a stand, takes a bill out of his pocket and flattens it for the machine's devouring. "For a minute you looked familiar, like the guy who married me."

"I look like your husband?"

"No. The man who performed the ceremony."

"Indeed?"

"You're about," Rachel says, "the same height, I guess."

"Not enough for identification," Reynard says, and looks—right—at—her. "They found a man early this morning down by Aquatic Park. Watch and wallet gone, face hammered to a pulp and scratches every which place. They still don't know who he is."

Martin steps back up the steps. The room is throttling with what was said, and the barman has not heard it but feels it. The juke plays a slumbery song that Rachel—Reynard caught the scent of this—used for comfort in her dorm room while a long-haired boy full of hashish and Ayn Rand terrorized her heart for a semester or so. Every pulse of hers rockets. Reynard sits back down and his body, his flesh, lays siege to her breath. The cover of the album has tribesmen carrying a snake across an urban backyard. By instinct Martin makes the drinks with lemon and caution, a gazelle eyeing a shadow on the plain.

"And how's the marriage?" Reynard asks, folding his hands over the cocktail napkin, which is stenciled with little tall trees.

"It's going *fine*," Rachel says. "Still married, very happy."

"It's wonderful to combine, isn't it?" Reynard asks her. "Melding lives, melding bodies. Till death or something do you part."

"Or *something*," Rachel says, like a hypnotized echo.

"Yes," Reynard says. "I wonder what that could be."

Martin plunks them down, shimmery lowballs nursing big craggy ice cubes. "Sazeracs." He'd made Rachel's as weak as he could get away with. Reynard downs most of his and looks at the ceiling while his belly—Martin and Rachel can almost *see* it in his shirt—purrs with it, some sleeping creature in its lair. Rachel is repulsed and drinks to forget it. Yet his eyes on her. Yet his hands on hers. Yet his face, more and more unshaven with every, what is happening, single second, his mouth moving and orange inside, yet, yet, yet.

"What is it?" he asks her.

He says this new startling thing like he's continuing a conversation, but then she answers it like one, too. "I married him," she says, "and everything sweet about him is irritating sometimes."

"Well, that's awful."

"There's project management—"

"Worse than that."

"—so he's gone, at work, all the time, and I don't know how to spend the rest of it," she says. "They won't increase my *hours* past part-time. So there's the other part of the time. I can only do the gym so much, a book with too much fancy coffee, and then I just *wait*."

Reynard widens his eyes and they're something in a planetarium, spinning and starry. She moves into orbit. "What are you waiting for?"

"I get scared," she says, "all the time."

"I can take your time away," Reynard tells her.

Martin clinks a bottle cleaning up, on purpose. Rachel backs out a little. "What are you talking about, what do you mean?"

"I think you need something inside you," Reynard says. "Smells like your husband isn't the right one. You need something wild and toothy."

"I don't think we're talking about the same thing."

"No," Reynard says, "we *definitely* are."

She reaches behind her, her fingers moving slow and useless, then down in front where the bar has little hooks, for a sweater if she brought one. "I have to go."

"I'll go with you."

"I'm going home."

He is leaning very close and talks like he's memorized it, a set of rules or an eternal prayer, right quick to her worried face. "We could go to anyone's home. My boot through the window, gone in a flash before the owners get back. What are you afraid of?"

"A large horse," she says, automatically, and for the first time.

"I know all about that." Reynard's murmur is like a lizard through the door. "I'll lick you right on your own neck. We don't even need a house. There's a field, a copse—"

Martin moves quick, wondering what the fuck all this is. There's sloppy pickups in bars, dangerous even, all the time under his watch, but this is penny-dreadful material the way this man is moving. He might as well be twirling a long waxed mustache, and for a jumpy moment, right when Reynard darts back a glance at the barman, he is. Then his face is clean-shaven and his eyes like the desperate and famished. There is no fire extinguisher for desire, but Lord knows, Martin thinks, there should be. Wall-mounted in every bedroom and watering hole, in all public buildings starting in seventh grade, under every wedding canopy, IN CASE OF EMER-GENCY BREAK GLASS. This, whipped up in seconds, will have to do.

"Try this," Martin says, also to himself. "Try these. New thing. Down the hatch. Hallowed Spirits whiskey, in a quick shot with some Athens ouzo and a local Fernet."

Rachel turns her face to face him. Her expression is that of, I was dreaming of eating marshmallows and now I am awake and my pillow is gone. "What is it?"

"Calling it Eye of Newt," the barman riffs.

"Don't listen to him," Reynard says, but Rachel already has the drink in her hands.

"The name's not final, it's true," Martin says, right to her. Her eyes are starlit and her mouth is already open.

"Let's get some air," Reynard says, standing up and cloaking.

"Slam it down," the barman says gently, and Mrs. Nickels does so. It's barking strong, a punch in every gut. The men watch the drink work through her like ink in the bath. She startles, stands and totters. Martin is around the bar to catch her before Reynard has a chance.

"Oh, dear," Reynard says, like there's vomit on the sidewalk.

"I've got her," the barman says. "This happens."

"Guess you shouldn't have given her that drink."

Rachel groans and passes way out. Martin has her full weight and watches one shoe waver off her foot. "It's a life of regret," he says.

Reynard bends down and retrieves, there it is, her sweater, a dainty thing of buttons and stitching. Both men imagine it being torn off, it already looks that way, in Reynard's clawish hand. "Not in my experience," the ghost says, and Martin quickly leans at him, almost a lunge, still holding Rachel by the shoulders. Reynard does not hiss and rear back, he does nothing vampiric or lycanthropic, he does not vow, eyes blazing, that he has not and will never be defeated before vanishing in choking black smoke that will rise out of Bottle Grove's door into a dark pillar making villagers shiver for miles around. But it sure seems like it. It really does, to Martin, who heaves his arms under Rachel so it's less like dragging a rug and more like carrying a maiden, such as a shiny knight or a giant ape might do, and makes his way with her down the spiral staircase. The purse scatters, the other shoe drops. Stanford watches, dumbstruck and struck dumb, until Martin is panting with her in the speakeasy.

"*Jesus,*" Stanford says.

"Boy oh boy," Martin says, and lays her out on the big wooden table, "do they walk amongst us." Her head lolls. "Do we have something for her to be comfortable? Some horse blankets?"

"Horse blankets?" Stanford repeats. "Oh, sure. The boot-black left some last time he was here for a flagon of ale."

It's the lingering spell of whoever that was, Martin thinks, what he just said. What *is* a copse, anyway? He just sees a wild place, or just a wild feeling. "That guy," he says out loud, "you fucked and his wife got furious."

Stanford runs a hand over his hair. "You'll have to be more specific."

"At the wedding."

"The vicar?"

"He," Martin says, "was no vicar."

Stanford has put the box down and puts a very strong and toned arm on Martin's. "What happened?" he asks quietly.

"He was going to hurt her."

"Wait, the vicar did *this*?"

"Maybe, or it wasn't him. I thought I recognized him and then, it was just a man his height."

"Martin, what are you talking about?"

"He had her, I don't know how to put it."

"Try."

"*In thrall.* So I slipped her some ouzo."

"Wait, what?"

"Among other things," Martin says, looking at her. The skirt is up a little, from moving her onto the table, but to reach over and tug it down would be dirtier, worse. "She was overserved."

"Wait, so *you* did this?"

"I passed her out, basically, yeah."

"Wait."

"Stop saying *wait*. I couldn't. There wasn't time."

They both look at her, two men in a boarded-up basement.

"It was a rescue," Martin says. "You should have seen it. He was like a fucking *monster* on her. Believe me, it's very, *very* I tell you, bad."

Stanford's hand is right there where he put it, on the barman. Their blood pulses together, like an underground spring. "OK cap'n," Stanford says, "I believe you, so now what?"

•

Padgett longs for an Old-Fashioned, fizzy on top with the fruit in a muddled swamp below. She misses Martin, she does. Instead she is way across town, boutiquey and skinny with little dogs, where everywhere is sushi but nobody is Japanese. She wears a sweater that should, from the price of it, be made of hundred-dollar bills, and she is looking over Nina's shoulder, through the window painted with the name of the place they're at, a name she can't remember and can't read tipsy.

A bottle of white is finished and the waiter, whom they have asked to do this or whom they haven't, is wiping it dry from the ice bucket and pouring tasters of the new identical bottle into clean glasses, making six pieces of glassware, if you count their untouched waters, for the two of them. Plus wine all day, Padgett thinks, remembering the blur of Kitsune's little napping face. By evening she will be as tired as a slumber party after-morning. They are, Nina is, talking about boys.

"He was unreliable," she says, blinking down at the two wines. It's a chalky white, because of the minerals in the soil of, Padgett looks at the label, *Italy*. She is unusual among tech girlfriends for snubbing California wineries, which the men are all buying. "Unreliable as in the sentence *You didn't show up, you fucking fuck*."

"And *fake*, right?" This new bottle, and knowing they will finish it, has tossed Nina's story into the brambles, and Padgett hopes they are still talking about the guy she is pretty sure they are talking about. "A fake vicar?"

"A fake *everything*," she says. "Crashes my car and is gone. And next day . . ." But then she moves her hand flat across the air, in a weird silence. Whatever she is not saying, she has said it several times. She keeps starting, "Next day," and then cuts off short, as if pricked by a thorn. She and Padgett have become, Padgett guesses you'd have to say, *friends*, but the friendship hasn't made room for much besides laughter and wine, so this story of Nina's keeps vanishing. "But *you*," Nina says now, "*you* were with the *bartender*."

They both howl a little at this hilarious unspeakable thing. It feels worse than nights with the Vic, pretending to have come to her senses and dumped Martin. "Free drinks, at least," Padgett says weakly.

"They're free *now*," Nina says, tipping more into her glass. "We're not party girls anymore, Padgett. I mean, bury me for a minute. *Bear.* With me. I was always *at minimum* a medium-sized nuisance to my parents."

"Yes," Padgett says, thinking of her faraway bedroom, likely still stilled like Pompeii.

"Went through college in a puff of smoke. Bad choices, or whatever you want to call those guys. Landing at the end of my overspent twenties with a monster of a guy who disappeared with most of my wallet."

The wine takes over for both of them, just a few seconds.

"And next day," Padgett prompts.

"Forget *next day*," Nina says, with a flitty wrist. "I land, not just on my feet but, who would think, on very wealthy territory. We're the same, Padgett, you're just like me. And we're out of the woods."

Nina's eyes are glittery, and her ring finger. She is marrying hers, a fleshy man who can't stop talking—Padgett in fact met him at the speakeasy party, although she remembers little more than a story about Bolivians who got kidnapped—in tech too, of course. His role is sneakier, more backgrounded than the Vic's. He works in private, helping things go public, and after a smattering of giddy dates, it's Padgett's understanding that he thinks Nina, elegant and fun, is the way to go. Padgett guesses she hopes they'll both be happy. Happy appears to be what they want, the way victims of airline disasters, on inflatable boats in a nowhere ocean with not enough supplies, also want to be happy. "Out of the woods," the fiancée repeats. "What about you?"

"It's going well," Padgett says.

"Better than bartending, I'm sure. But you're breastfeeding the little baby and he's not marrying you yet?"

"It's not *breastfeeding*," Padgett says, but it's the *yet* that gets her. "I'm happy," she tries. They are facing each other, but it feels like two secrets, two fortune-telling cards facedown.

"What is it?" Nina says. "You can tell me, Padgett. There's something you're scared of, I can smell it. A sex thing? I've heard all of *that*, from my old roommate who makes movies in the old Armory. Does he hit you? Bad drugs? Can't be that, you'd like any drug he could find. He needs another baby? You can hire that out."

"Animal proteins," Padgett says, before she can stop herself, the first she has spoken of this out loud. She promised she would never, and she breaks the promise *here*, at the Brasserie What's-it?

Nina is frowning and refilling. "What? Cosmetic something? Is he making you—"

Padgett shakes her head. It's easiest to keep a secret when it's drowned and forgotten. Something about synapses being quick, quicker than anything electronic. The Vic was flushed as a teenager monologuing about it while the cage rattled. "They're testing a thing," she says. "In a building. In a basement. It scares me."

"Scares you what? Scares you how?"

"He has secrets."

"They all do, Padgett. One thing you do not want in life with a man, is to know his secrets. I'd eat ground glass before I checked Gabe's browser history."

"A basement," Padgett hears herself saying. "*Animals.*"

Nina looks wild with wine. "That's *it*! That's the same. Wild. I can't even describe."

"I don't know if we're talking about the same thing."

"No, we *definitely* are."

Padgett holds up wine in a solitary toast: *Your turn, then.* Nina sighs. "When Reynard and I were in the accident?"

A kid on the diving board just needs a push. "Next day," Padgett says, again again, and this time it takes.

"Next day my neighbor's home is broken into, his apartment, and I mean *broken*. And he's *killed*. This firefighter the next day, very handsome if you like muscular, told me the fixtures were all busted up, holes in the walls, and that the medical whoever told *him* it was like the guy had his *stomach scooped out*."

Nina looks at her, *How do you like that?*, and Padgett figures they're all, everyone on this grayed-in planet, drunk as skunks. "OK," she says.

Nina shakes her head like a tennis match. "Not OK. It's been boarded up but I think someone's living there."

"Like, squatters?"

"Not *squatting*. Scratching around. It's why I gave up on my place and just moved in with Gabriel almost instantly."

"Sure, this is why you abandoned a scroungy Sunset apartment for some huge Noe Valley—"

"Not *scroungy*. But I was afraid they were going to *break through*."

"Break through where?"

Nina just shakes her head. "When I went one last time back to pick up my last stuff, there was a guy coming out, very tall. For a second I thought it was Reynard. He had something all banged up with him, a motorcycle helmet I think, but he was carrying it like a bowl, and I swear to God, Padgett, it looked like it was *full* of *bloody meat*."

She looks at Padgett again, and Padgett drinks wine again.

"I must have made a noise," Nina says, "and the guy, I shouldn't say *guy*, looks up." She leans across the table, almost tipping the tall delicate glasses to the floor. The place is filling up, it's time for everybody to drink now. "It made me run. I ran six blocks with him behind me in the rain. I fell into a planter, Padgett, I was a mess, outside Martin's bar. They got me a hot toddy because of what I saw when he turned around."

Padgett can't help it, whatever expression she is displaying. She lifts her glass and that, too, rings a faint bell. "What?"

"He had, I am telling you, an animal face. A real animal. The face of a fox. Oh Padgett, I'm frightened, actually. I really am." Nina leans in with her slaphappy eyes. "They're everywhere, Padgett. The city's changing. Men, *beasts* like this are prowling around all over the place like it's theirs."

"Nina," Padgett says, "I'm not sure I'm sure what you're talking about."

"I think you are," Nina says. She reaches out, first for Padgett's hand and then for the wine bottle, which she grips to her chest like it's a weapon at the ready, or maybe just something she doesn't want to share. "Padgett, you know what you ought to do?"

Padgett brushes back her bangs. Across the room, the waiter thinks she's asking for the bill. It's not quite a question, what Nina has asked, and yet Padgett doesn't know the answer. She looks at the muddle in front of her, all this drink on this fancy table, the pricey neighborhood outside, everything rising like a flood. Martin, where are lonely you? "What," she asks blearily, "should I ought to do?"

"Get married," this woman tells her. "Before it's too late."

CHAPTER 5

*G*O HOME, THE streetlights say to Rachel. For weeks now she's been creeping around her neighborhood at night, reminding herself of the doomed girls in gory movies, alone and unprotected from fangs and chainsaws and what have you. In this case, nothing. *Go home*, but she doesn't. She's pregnant. She can't drink and doesn't want to eat, she's tired but can't sleep, she's growing a baby but not always sure she wants a family. She's a woman alone on the streets, but her rovings take her no place but the long-asleep residential blocks and one little business patch. Here's the grocery store that never seems to carry anything. Here's the palm reader she visited once years ago, with other drunk bridesmaids, where for seventy-five dollars she learned everything was going to be fine. Here's the big lopsided Victorian, a fallen cake that she's heard is an assisted-living center, where a woman sits each morning in the lobby, brandishing a rolled-up magazine over her knobby knees. And here's the Kitsune School—an early education place her kid would likely attend someday, given its location and well-purchased reputation—and—

There's a man on top of the building.

He's between two solar panels, crouched down or seated, hooded. If she sees him, he must certainly see her. Like a gargoyle he waits there, and for a moment Rachel thinks that must be what he is, something the Kitsune children made together, an art project to decorate the roof, a papier-mâché something to fool passersby, like the plastic owls that spook pigeons away. It's not that, though. The building is just two stories tall, close enough that Rachel can see the pulse of breath under his hooded garment. Is that possible? It seems so, alone at night. For a moment it, the man, looks perched to leap down upon her, and Rachel strains for what to do besides perish here, on a foolhardy walk, a foolhardy victim. But then she watches it rise to an upright position and walk carefully to the edge—and then, terrifyingly, the man's body swings itself off and begins to climb down the drain-pipe, steady and with very little creaking. The arms move wide and slender, as if the man were swinging from tree to tree. Rachel steps out of the circle of light and runs, runs. She runs past the lobby of the Victorian, empty but lit, and considers hurrying up the creaky-looking steps to pound on the glassy doors, but she's seen that movie too: cornered against a building, or the man on the roof is harmless but past the doors is a pack of violent cannibals.

So she keeps at it with the fleeing, her breath rasping hot in her mouth and her feet clopping and clopping, until it seems the man is chasing her on the back of a horse he has managed to find. She will lose the baby, she worries, from running and fear. It's a little baby, so little it's not even a baby. Onscreen she read it's the size of a lipstick, but, Rachel knows franti-cally, she loses lipsticks *all the time*. They fall out of her purse

like lemmings, and now she is at the front door of her house—
bungalow, is what they call it, but the word sounds so fragile
that she knows the terrifying man will tear it apart, like a boy
with a box. Why did she run here and lead this galloping beast
to her home? She could at least have saved her boring husband.
She is ringing and ringing the doorbell with one hand and
trying to wrest the keys out of her pocket with the other.
A tissue and a lipstick fall out—*see?*—and then the door is
open, her husband shocked in sweatpants with his hair tufted
out like an infant bird, one hand bookmarking a copy of
The Expecting Book, the bible all expectant women read, and
he looks so dazed and concerned that she throws herself into
his arms. The book drops and she sobs a little on his shoulder
and kicks back with her foot, slamming the door, she is
certain, on the rampaging nose of her terrible pursuer.

"What?" Ben is saying over and over. "What, sweetie?
What? What?"

"There's a man," she is able to say, "on top of the Japanese
school."

They're quiet for a minute, and Rachel, still clinging to her
husband, can hear the tick of his mother's loud clock, surren-
dered when she moved to Arizona. Ben reaches over her to
click the locks locked. Sensible of him, she thinks, and life-
saving. "He was chasing me."

"Start over," he suggests, and gentle-arms her into the
living room. His tossed-away blanket, a steaming mug on the
little table, the props he has from staying up waiting for her,
now waiting for them both. She sits where he was sitting, the
cushions still warm from his bulk, and shivers. "I couldn't
sleep again," she says, "so I was walking—"

"You know you panic me when you do that."

"I know," she says.

"I had to get up just to wait for you."

"OK, but there was a man—" She shivers again and grabs Ben's mug for a sip. He starts to say something, and doesn't say something. It's a toddy in her mouth, heavily honeyed but God Almighty the taste of whiskey when she's given up drinking, even watered down she drinks it like she's suckling. "On top," she says, wiping her mouth with her sleeve, "of the Japanese school."

"There was alcohol in that, you know."

"*Ben.*"

"There *was.* I'm sorry. It's midnight and you're talking, all I'm picturing is a pagoda."

She has to laugh at this. Maybe it's only a little tipsiness, her tolerance way down from ten weeks of, basically, sobriety. He smiles too. "The school," she says. "You know, the one the Vic started."

"He didn't really start it, but yeah, right by that shitty grocery where I bought the peas."

She looks hard at him and gets out of the chair. They are standing together in the middle of the room. If this story is about two couples, two marriages, this surely is one of them. "You did?"

"That rainy day," he reminds her, "when the rain chased us out of the park. You had a craving, pea soup."

"I *did,*" she says, in considerable amazement, remembering his soaked face in the kitchen, holding out the can like a trophy.

"But there was a man?"

"He was hiding up there."

Her husband is really trying to follow this. "Why would he be hiding?"

"Why would anyone? And then he was shimmying down."

"Shimmying?"

"They always say that about drainpipes," she says glumly. Now the whole story is getting swept someplace, the terror of her midnight street-walk just particles to be brushed away with a broom, not worth worrying over. It's mutual. She is helping her husband decide that it was nothing.

"So after he shimmied away from the solar panels?"

"I was just scared, is all," she says, and she lets this spread around them, the *is all*, and she feels the toddy in her belly, gurgling around the baby. Let it have a sip, let them all calm down. She was frightened, is all, she thinks, tell him this. Or else tell him what? This is a man in whom she has complete if reckless confidence, who will believe, basically, anything she tells him, at midnight at least. So what can she tell him?

"When I was a little girl," she says, "I saw a really creepy horse."

It's like the wind is rising, outside the bungalow, but everything still stands. Of course it stands. There was not a horse outside, not tonight in a residential neighborhood in San Francisco. There was a man, maybe, but there are men everywhere. Right here for instance, listening to her as best he can.

"I think it had something wrong with its neck," Rachel tells him, "or maybe it was just a creepy species."

This must be how Ben nods when he's in a meeting. "Breed."

"Breed!" she says. "Yes! Thank you! A decorative neck, I guess. Decorative, or cancer. But it scared me and"—she sighs, because here is where she would order or pour another drink, before this baby cock-blocked that strategy—"I think about it all the time."

He nods again but then thinks better of that and hugs her, right on schedule. "Oh, honey."

"I never told you," she says. "I never told anyone," and decides to fool herself, not just him, that she was too drunk to remember that time she told a weird guy in a bar in the afternoon. In fact, maybe it did not happen, maybe she made that up, just a foggy whiskey dream, waking up on, what was it, a table, in a basement room with curtains but no windows.

"Ssh," he says. "You poor thing."

"Yes, I am," she says. "I took a walk and got scared and thought about the horse—"

"Ssh."

"I don't want Nicky going to that school."

"Who's Nicky?"

"Our baby maybe."

His body tenses a little against her, like they'll discuss that later, when she remembers her last name is Nickels. "Ssh. You know what I think? You know what scares me?"

"That I spent like four months drinking in a bar while you worked late?" she does not say. This rises up in her every so often, not just in her but surely, she thinks, in women all over town. Countless husbands' risings in tech have left educated, capable women in confusing shade, and then they get pregnant. But she does not say anything.

"My wife scares me," Ben says, "wandering the streets at night. It makes me wake up and think like a horror movie."

"But I can't sleep."

"Wake me up, if you can't sleep."

"But that's the *opposite*," she tells him. "Then you'll be cranky at work. And what are we going to do—"

"Have sex," Ben says.

"Right!" she says. "Yes! Breed! Thank you!"

They both laugh and kiss, both honey-breathed and happy to be embracing rather than worrying about the roof of a Japanese school. They would do it on the floor but he never likes to, he always leads her, no matter how naked, to the white expanse of the bed, pulls back the cover so they have the whole empty field to play on. So they go there, and the ghost of the fox, too, moves around the bungalow, on the outside, from the shrubbery outside the living room to a twitchy tree, its forked trunk long and high enough for him to crawl along it and press his flickering face against the bedroom window.

•

Her breath when she kisses me.
Laying around afterwards.
Stop thinking about it.
More late shifts alone? Ask Stanford.
Pistachio infusion?
Amaro and mescal—
Do. Not. Call. Padgett.

Stanford moves his hand in front of Martin's list like he's washing a window. Martin blinks out of it. "You," Stanford says, "are coming, *right now*, to a rolling stop at the line past which a bartender cannot drink. And Martin, that's a generous leash."

Martin lays his arm on top of the legal pad, way too late, so Stanford won't see all the sad items he's been cataloging. "I am trying new recipes," he says, listening to his own unsteadiness. "Mixing. I am attempting things for the menu."

Stanford plucks a bottle of Armagnac out of Martin's reach, slowly, like he's showing him how to do it, and dings a finger on a tall untouched club soda. "This is a Tuesday," he says, and gestures around the bar. One guy's nursing his last at the far end, and that's it. "A workday and a worknight. You have mail you should be opening, with bills we must, must, must try to pay."

Martin looks down at his list, like it's something he dropped and broke. "Gay men have it so easy," he says.

"My mother hasn't spoken to me in nine years."

"Still."

Now Stanford presents Martin with a mug of coffee, his hands gently cupped. "Still nothing. Sober up. We have to move careful in this town, Martin. It is full of wicked money and not enough of it plunked down here. Rents are rising. There are many watering holes already doing better. I will lose the venture of this bar, OK, but I will not lose it to your bullshit."

Martin sips frownily. "To be fair," he tries, "your mother hasn't spoken to me in nine years either."

Stanford decides to smile it off and bumps his fist against Martin's mug. The two men met serving drinks at a large franchise that dreamt itself elegant. They had not much in common aside from thinking, back then, that they could run a place better. They have comraded themselves, helped along by the professional knowledge, learned early to anyone slinging liquor, that you cannot argue with a drunk dude.

"I can't stand this grind," Martin says.

"You mean blend."

"Well," Martin says, "I'm realizing, my theory is, that I just don't like coffee." He puts the mug down, gives it up.

"Why don't," Stanford says quietly, "you just stop thinking about her."

Martin lifts, very drunkenly, the pen from behind his ear and underlines Padgett's name. There are six other underlines there. There's girl problems on the jukebox too—Hank Williams, always sad about something even though he was clearly a lout. "I'm sorry," Stanford says. "I know if anyone had the trick to figuring how to stop thinking about the person stomping all over your totally, in your case, innocent heart, they'd clear one billion dollars easy."

"Only if they put it on a phone," Martin says.

"I agree that tech bros are part of your problem, yes."

"You don't know the half of it," Martin says to Stanford, because he doesn't. Martin imagines the mountain of money, an actual billion in coins piled up in some overlord's cave, but his girl, his sharp lovely girl, is dating the goddamn overlord.

"I'm sorry," Stanford says again. "When I go home and my cat—"

"You have a cat?"

"You've met the cat."

"I thought the cat left with what's-his-name last year."

"Davey and I got the cat together," Stanford says.

"*Davey*, I could never get used to that."

"And we agreed at the split-up that the cat would go to whoever was doing less drugs at the time."

"What are you saying, with the cat."

"Forget it now. It was a story, and the point is—"

"The point is—?"

"When she's chasing her tail," Stanford says, "she is still, even when she's never going to catch it, having a good time," and Padgett walks into Bottle Grove. Stanford shoots God a look of *Are you kidding me?* and offers a quick trade, rejected, of another year of silence from his mother for the girl to disappear in a puff of smoke. No dice, she walks right up to the bar. Martin is staring like it's the first time he's seen an elephant. She walks OK, nowhere near as drunk as Martin is, but one arm hangs limp and useless like someone's severed the nerve. She practically has to lift it with the other hand to plunk it down in front of Martin. It's the left one, with a very large diamond on a ring on the ring finger.

"I'm going to excuse myself to the basement," Stanford says, "with my cigarette lighter and a bunch of gasoline-soaked rags."

He stomps off. The guy in the corner catches the vibe and scoots out, a nighttime appointment having been invented and remembered. Martin grabs a towel and wipes something with it, doesn't matter what, very busy at the moment, busy busy. "How are you?" he says.

"Just walked out of a restaurant," Padgett says, "threw my new phone into a gutter while I signaled the car with the light from this ring before I jumped out without paying, six blocks ago. I guess I'm impulsive."

"And I guess congratulations are in order," he says, without looking up.

"No, no," Padgett corrects him fiercely. "Don't blame you on me. *You're* the one. This was *your* idea."

"I know."

"Then don't—"

"I know. It's like a sticky note nailed to my forehead. I thought of it."

"And it's happened, Martin. The Vic just asked me to marry him. I am here, I covered my goddamn tracks, to talk about it. *You* were the one who said, you goddamn did, to go after him. It is a comment under the album on that stupid music site, *Grab the brass ring*, so don't deny you wanted this."

Martin walks over to the mail, another thing to park his eyes in front of. "What I said," he says, "was not how it was you said I said it."

Padgett's shiny ring is still on her finger on the bar, like it's picking up the tab tonight. "What?"

"I don't know." Martin faces her then, looks at the same adroit face, distrustful and askance, that made his heart swell, that *interested* him so, since the wedding where they met. "Did you say yes?" he asks, and opens an envelope.

"This was *your* plan."

"I'm just asking."

"It wasn't time to say yes. He told me to think about it, and I raced out of the place."

Martin has read a letter with a small, boyish smile, and tears it up over the garbage can, a very little blizzard in just one place. "And?"

"And I told you where I threw the phone, Martin. It's a prototype. It's thousands of dollars if you can even get one. And you can't. He's going to kill me."

"Just say you were all aflutter."

"Why," Padgett says, "are you so mad at me, that you are *not* pouring me a drink?"

He gets to it, a crashy chop-chop in an efficient sulk. From her stool Padgett can't tell what he's doing exactly, muddled ginger maybe, or some special sugar blend. But when it's served up in front of them, it's just two shots of Irish whiskey and two lines of cocaine, veering across the little plate like disputed boundary lines.

"Martin, *no.*"

"What?"

"I promised Vic I wouldn't."

"*The* Vic."

"You don't call him that. For the baby, I promised."

"*Jesus*, you're pregnant?"

"The baby he *already* has, you idiot."

Martin does the line like a snuffling dog.

"And you," Padgett says, "already look fucked up."

"Well," Martin says, "my girlfriend is getting married. Doesn't happen every day."

"Not girlfriend," Padgett says, her voice rising, "not breast-feeding and not *married*, not yet."

"There's that *yet*," Martin says, sipping whiskey.

"Look, I'm trying to tell you the truth. I'm going back and forth on it."

"Mostly forth, I bet."

"Why are you spitting at me like this? This is what we did. This is what we planned." She performs the slouch everybody gets at a bar, sooner or later: *What am I doing here?*

"And if I asked you to," Martin says, "give him up, to come back with me—"

Padgett swipes away a little bit, just a little, of crying. "And sit here at the bar with you and the jukebox."

Martin gestures to the drinks, the drugs, the sticky surface. "This is nothing new. You liked it *then*."

"*Martin.*"

"Is it just *money*? The reason you—"

"This was *yours*," Padgett says again. "Con him out, you said. Marry him, money for everybody. It is *so. Much. Money*, Martin, but it's not something you can steal like that, and neither is he."

"It's socked away."

"No, not *socked*. Money now, in this day and whatever, is the *idea* of it."

"No, only rich people say that. I have to purchase the liquids in these bottles with actual, like from my wallet—"

"Not for him," Padgett says, shaking her head, her whole body, the ring catching the light. "Not when it's like this. The money is in what he does, they move it from place to place, like a hat trick, and conning him, marrying him for the money, it's another complicated thing. They're about to pull a scheme where everybody will have to buy their music, *everybody*, all over again."

The jukebox spins a little Leadbelly, as if to say, *Not me*. The mood breaks from it. Martin and Padgett smile, barely. "On the other hand," he says, and holds up his other hand. There's a wrinkled check in it, from the envelope, anachronistic in its typing and some weird texture on the paper of it. Padgett tries to look calmly at it, but the argument is still shaking in her hands, particularly the ring finger, and her heart's beating with its rapid transit.

"Public transportation," says Martin Icke, "bought me a shoe."

"Wow."

"Long time ago, I know. Not very punctual. It took three letters to BART and a phone call."

"OK."

"And you thought I'd never amount to anything," Martin says, but the drugs, and his sadness, are hindering the deadpan. He just sounds actually unhappy.

"Well, I'm glad."

"A new shoe," he says. "A mate for the lonely single one at home."

"Please stop."

"Please drink with me," Martin says. "Stay a little. Do the line."

She thinks of the sad little parade he wants, children and piñatas. Her heavy hand picks up the glass.

"You drink a lot," Martin says.

"I do," she says, drinking a little.

"Well, they say marriage is a civilizing influence."

"*Marriage*," she says, and the barman raises his glass to clink.

"Marriage," he says.

"But on the other hand, *marriage*."

"Yeah," Martin says. "I hear that too. What are you going to do, Gail Padgett?"

"I don't know, Vic."

And the song ends. "Um," Martin says.

"*Martin*. There's lots to decide. He said to think it over, and then there's lawyers and stuff."

"To sock the money away."

"I'd still have," she says, "money. A very lot of it. There's just, you know, strings."

They both picture the lawyers opening briefcases in unison, taking out large balls of string and getting to work like spiders.

"Well, there's your decision," he says.

Padgett puts down her half-finished drink, and then, what the hell, finishes it. A decision is like a guitar, Padgett thinks. She doesn't know how to make one.

Martin looks over at her. They met at a wedding, and in every wedding is the makings of another. He takes her hand, keeps looking, and when she finally looks back, she can see herself, and that's all, in each of his eyes.

"Just," he says, his mouth slouchy with drink, "just tell me that you still love me."

"Martin."

"With your *eyes*," he says. "At least. If you can't say it."

They have never said they loved each other. They have said they loved Manhattans, and lounging under a cloud of them, on an unmade bed noisy with nearby television. They have said they love the sound of the M Ocean View train on foggy afternoons, all creaky on the dampened tracks, or maybe they didn't say that, just listened to it from the kitchen floor. To say she still loves him, *still*, before she said she loves him at all, is chaser first. Yet Martin. Yet his eyes on her, hanging himself on any word she will say. Tell him what?

"As God is my witness," she says, and although she has the feeling God is nowhere near this empty room, there's something *there*. She can hear it, in the dark past the bar's glow, she can feel it, but if it's god or man, a creature or a ghost or the line of cocaine she leans over to inhale and seal the deal, she does not, falling into blackout, cannot know.

•

Something happens then, or it happened later, and then she's half come to. Her arms ache from holding up the little blue chair that she remembers forcing, bumpity bump, under the doorknob to jam it all, against some creature, some animal lost in the howling liquor.

Her room, her old bedroom, is a wreck. Who let her sleep in this wreckaged wreck? The bed has been over, the mattress slabbed up against a shelf and the sheet fitted over just one corner, with a stain in the shape of a stain. But it's not like she's been sleeping in it. Padgett is here on the floor, with a little blanket, stitched with baby animals.

She stretches and is not wearing pants. It is not the first time she has lost time. It is, she thinks, the scariest. There's a scratch down her leg, the way she used to go crazy on her own body. Her mother, she remembers, thank God, is at a chamber music festival in New Hampshire, is where she is, OK, there's some time, you have time to piece back the blacked-out shambles. Wind comes in through the broken window, and instead she could live in a palace. Her spirits are low, and everything she can get her hands on wobbles in the middle of the bedroom trying to get some sort of grip. The lifeline is where, the rescue is what. Listening for something, is what she's doing.

The answer is *yes*.

She slips to her childhood bathroom, floss and gloss in the cabinet, and throws up. Her legs go back in her underwear and back in her pants, like cream in coffee. At least this will be done. The hallway down to her childhood kitchen exhibits what the police would call *signs of a struggle*. Let's not call them, no, let's not summon the police to your mother's house to hear from you that you do not know what has happened to you, if something did.

It doesn't matter. She gets there. The Vic's place has a flat garden, grassless since the days of drought, full of black rocks and a fountain that always makes her want to pee, but that's not where the door is that insiders use. That's the one with the clattery stairs along the side, and by the time Padgett reaches the top, her heart is so thumpy and loud it's like she's being chased by somebody. She has no idea what time it is, maybe ten, with birds chirping. She bams on the door.

The Vic opens up, and the scene behind him is so peaceful it's deflating. Kitsune is in a wooden high chair, just kicking around, and the Vic is in a baggy Scandinavian garment his marketing head brought him back from a conference, somewhere between pajamas and what a wizard would don. A harmless perk of music is going on, and there's a sandwich, inched out of its wrapping, on a blue plate.

"Hi."

"Hi."

Padgett steps in. "How am I doing on time?"

There's a clock from Scandinavia too, on the plain white wall, or maybe from Hayes Valley in their own city. Civilization is overrated, Padgett thinks, looking at the silverware, but what else is there? Vic, meanwhile, is alarmed a little. "What happened to you? You look—are you OK?"

She sits down at the table, just out of kicking range from the baby. "You told me to think about it, to take my time."

"That was two days ago," the Vic says. "The Trail found your prototype in a *gutter.*"

Two days ago would explain why she is so hungry. He follows her gaze to the sandwich. "It's from the Vietnamese place," he says. "Have a bite. Have a whole half. I'll make you some tea."

Padgett shivers. "Toddy," she manages to croak, but the Vic shakes his head.

"No," he says, and Kitsune says something like "no" too.

"I said *totally,*" Padgett amends, but the Vic is still shaking his head. He shakes it for a while.

"No," the Vic says again, and the music turns bland and zippy, with a swinging trumpet, not his sort or hers. "Padgett, I can't have you like this. Drinking and having fun are one thing. It's colorful. But this, Padgett, you like this is *wreckage.*"

Padgett is savoring *colorful.* It's the nicest synonym, the happiest way anyone has ever called her goddamn fucking nuts.

The baby makes a noise, like someone has walked into the room she hasn't thought of for years.

"It's not respectful," the Vic says, "to yourself."

"What am I listening to?"

"I'm trying to tell you—"

"No," Padgett says. "The music."

The Vic puts the tea down. It's steaming and the smell is smooth but complicated. Someone has taken time with it, the blend or grind or what have you. The Vic makes a noise, a gesture like he's done folding laundry, surely something he hasn't done in years. "I've been acclimating Kitsune to your favorite album."

"My favorite—?"

"Your Trail says you listen to this the most," the Vic says. "It wasn't even on my system. That was why, wasn't it? Your old laptop you kept keeping. Well, it is now."

It's the jazz record, the secret one. His eyes are not one bit implying he's decoded all her messages, so it's just a gift. Now she'll have to hear it forever, something she'll need to pretend to love.

If this story is about two couples, two marriages, which one is this, and who are they?

"Of course," the Vic says, his eyes sparkling sharp, "it means you'll have to pay to hear it. Everybody will."

"*Yes,*" Padgett tells him, but she sees he doesn't hear it, not for what it is. He tears off a piece of the sandwich bread, soaked with oil, and puts it on the tray of the high chair for his daughter to think about. The baby winces, and Padgett gets a flash of Martin Icke with one shoe, his more or less innocent face. What can she do for him? The answer to this is money.

"Why are you with me?" Padgett asks. "Aren't you afraid?"

The Vic's mouth is full of sandwich. "I'm not really afraid of anything," he says, and with slow wonder, Padgett, as women think about men so often, cannot believe how stupid he is. "If you meet me halfway," he says, "I think we can make this work."

"Halfway to *what*?" Padgett says.

"We get along," the Vic insists. "We *talk*, at the table. In bed. On the balcony. We tell each other things, the stories of things. I never had that with anybody except stoned and twenty."

Padgett feels her own eyes widen. She does not know any of this. Right now she does not remember a single moment with this man that would lead here.

"*Everyone*," she says, "if you marry me, will say you married too soon. I'll be, we both will be tilted like that. The *second wife*."

"They said that the first time," the Vic says. "Maureen got pregnant. We knew each other for something like *nothing*, no time at all."

"Really?"

"One of the things," the Vic says, feeding another chunk to the wary baby, "that I love, is that you don't read up on me much."

"Whereas *you*," Padgett says, "track my albums."

"It's the nature of the beast," the Vic says, and points at himself. "If it wasn't for you I'd be clambering all over everybody. It sounds, I know how it sounds, but marriage is a civilizing influence."

"Was it that for you?"

The Vic takes her hand, warm from the mug of tea. "It *will* be," he says.

"I mean with Maureen."

His face darkens. Padgett can feel something move from his hand to hers, not just pressure but something cracklier.

"What?" she asks him.

"You don't know this?"

"I *clearly*," she says, "don't know anything."

The Vic looks quick at the door, in sudden reverie or checking for spies. "Maureen and I," he says, "basically hated each other," and she feels it, a wave of emancipation as if some heavy bad roof were lifted and the wind can rush through her hair and furniture. Even the baby kicks, and now she can remember:

—"OK, I'll tell one," and the Vic blows a smoke ring—he's breezing through a box of cigars this week, gifted leftovers from a photo shoot—out into the sky from the balcony. Padgett stands with him, her hand in the back pocket of his jeans, which feels a little trashy.

"Goes like this," the Vic says. "First five weeks with our new CFO, every morning I'd put a little screw on his desk."

"What?"

"His office had a very old ceiling fan, Art Deco I think, the decorator found. Right over his desk. I grabbed random stuff from a hardware store, everything tiny, washers and screws and springs. Every morning, I'd leave one right in the middle of his desk."

"Was this a symbolic thing? *Screw you?*"

"It was not *symbolic*," the Vic says, as if the word were *genocide*. "I wanted to see what he would do, call maintenance, stand on the desk to try to fix the problem."

"And—?"

"And at the end of five weeks I had to sign for a registered package. Every screw in the bag, with a note saying, *I believe you dropped these.*"

Padgett takes her hand out. "How did he—?"

"No grease on them, maybe. They did look brand-new. I don't know, though, we never talked about it."

"Never?"

"It was never mentioned and he's still with us. Great guy."

A smoke ring fades into the dusk, a touch more pollution on the city lights. "*Great guy?* Is the word you would use—?"

"It's a *story*," the Vic says, and—

—Padgett has had five vodka tonics at the reception they breezed through. Now the bed is tilting houseboatily, but she's trying to listen.

"I was sixteen and she was twenty-three. Her dad was a market guy, I was interning or whatever you'd call getting coffee and yelled at."

Padgett knows *market* doesn't mean piles of grapes and onions, even though that's what she always pictures.

"Around the office they said she was engaged, straight out of Yale. She was odd and quiet but very smart, we rolled our eyes together at this bull-session brainstorm reception for a state senator, I think it was." He rolls over, away from Padgett. "I remember her skin looked blue almost, so pale, like the blood would just ripple out if you bit her cheek. I was eager to lose it, though. I was *so scrawny*, approaching a girl for sex felt like a noodle asking someone to the movies."

"You were sixteen," Padgett forgives him.

"Well, damn right. Somehow I'm in her apartment, it felt so grown-up, thirty floors up in the elevator, all these fuzzy rugs, and photographs everywhere of the two of them, this quiet girl and the grinning fratty fiancé, in tuxedos, on a boat,

some resort restaurant under an umbrella. We hardly spoke
or anything, just did it quick, and she tells me to leave. I figure
it's one last fling before the walk down the aisle, right?"

"Oh."

"No, the *oh* is next week or so, her dad mentions, *just so
the staff will know*, he died in some blizzard, the fiancé, some
avalanche in Colorado—I remember, I was so young it was
before I knew people skied there—like six months previous."

The Vic rolls back. His eyes are coaly, the least shiny eyes
Padgett has seen that weren't on a cave painting. "She wasn't
sexy," he says. "She wasn't *daring* anything. It was *grief.* She
was broken," and Padgett does not know whether to reach to
him or—

—flowers in a vase, why should they make her so furious, but
they do. Flowers in a vase and the vase is also from the florist,
heavy pineconed glass like a fairytale prom. The fancy
flowers are wrong for it, so fancy they're hardly flowers at all,
just spiky showpieces on nearly wooden stems. "It just seemed
time," the Vic is saying.

"Because *they* told you it was time," Padgett says, her fingers
on one of the thistly parts. Somewhere there was a wild field
full of these, an underpaid someone picking them for a reason
they couldn't guess, while she, also insensibly, is picking an
argument.

"Stop saying *they*," the Vic says. "I thought you could use
some flowers today."

"And what would I use them for?"

"For being happy," her boyfriend says instantly, and opens
his arms in the kitchen, too wide, slightly vaudeville.

"I don't like that you have a thing on a machine that tells you flowers, no-reason emails, what is it called?"

"No-reason emails is right."

"No, the notice system."

Vic looks away like a marble fell off the table, and they both wait for it to rattle into a lost corner. "Happy Couple," he admits. "Look, I'm taking a shower. I don't want to get into it. Throw away the flowers or treasure them forever."

"A treasure not from you," Padgett says. "It's from *them*. It's from your system."

"You are throwing rocks at a wasp's nest," he says, the phrase just a mess of hissing. "I. Am not. Getting into it."

"I want to *talk* about it," Padgett insists, although she does not appear, she notices, to be standing up as he walks away, already down the hall. There's an envelope of organics, to pour into the vase with the water, to keep them alive. "Vic—"

"Not getting into it," he calls back, cheerfully, and she hears the water run. She can tear open the envelope at least, roughly. She can spill it out, into the sink, over the trash, and then take down her own glass of wine while he gets clean. How many couples, a lot she guesses, are kept up by just not getting into it?—

—and she sees all these remembered scenes as if in a film montage interlaced with circling clocks and pattering calendars, and when she fades out of it the Vic is waiting for her line.

"Yes," she says.

He gives her a look. "What?"

"Yes," she says. "Yes, I will marry you."

His delight is immediate, yelping and profound. "You will?"

"Yes."

"When?"

"Um, someday." It is something she keeps deciding, like some long hard jog, when every step you could stop and instead walk sweaty and panting to a bar. She has a lifetime to make this choice; she will do it someday and she is doing it now. When he asks if she is serious, what else can she tell him, what else is there to say?

The word is *champagne*.

"*Yes*," Padgett says, and the baby kicks her feet, although lollygaggingly. She is fading fast. The Vic is looking for bubbly in his nearest refrigerator, but Padgett already knows where it is. And she is thinking of another wedding, a family wedding, in a lodge named after the family, hers. She was fourteen, and after a solemn ceremony bedecked with bagpipes, she wandered ignored in Bottle Grove. The man was, she thinks, a friend of her uncle's. The light was a perfect green, the greenest and most perfect light in her life, and although she can recall—recall or *invent*—his thick hands on her knees, this is not where she wants to return. Maybe he was a beast, and that was wrong. But what was right, magically and green, was the thrill in her mouth, dancing and locked inside her forever, just moments after he said, "And this, my dear, is vodka and orange juice."

Oh, the world is where you're flung, every day's an unfair gumball machine. She's here now, in a mansion that's not hers but to which—it is always the way with mansions—she is beginning to feel entitled. Padgett has the lion's share of champagne and begins nudging the Vic, who is talking about wineries, seasons, good clear weekends to invite people, with her scratched-up legs, still sore but healing up quick like good little scars. Her fiancé is talking quickly, like he does about tech, quick, she thinks, before she changes her mind. His silly garment comes open a little, at her burrowing feet.

"I love you," he says, and she kisses him in reply. They rise and put the baby down, and they go into the bedroom and three years pass.

Part Two

CHAPTER 6

A MAN IN his thirties walks into a bar. This isn't a joke. Half past five on a school day, and it's quiet in the place like it's time to turn the record over and play the other side. Bottle Grove is still the name of the establishment, and the name of the man who runs it is still Martin Icke. He pushes the man's ID card back to him without looking at it. "I've seen you in here before," he says.

"Yes?" The man looks around like he doubts it.

"Think so," Martin says. "I remember the picture."

"Maybe," the man says, and maybe he's right. The man is in a limp green jacket, which he tablecloths over a barstool before unwinding at length a very long skinny scarf from his scruffy neck. This, and the quick careless order from the list of fancy local beers, does a job of presenting him, to no real audience but the barman, as basically a nice guy. He is not any nice guy. This is Reynard, trying a new tack. Prowling, holing up, stalking and leaping upon them—these are activities pushed to the back burner. He's grown a beard, stopped drinking—the barman starts the tap—got himself colored contact lenses and a job at a progressive preschool. He's cool now. They say if you meet someone again under different circumstances, they might as well be a different person. Clean up a man and he is marriage material, and then of course marriage is, further, a civilizing influence. Reynard is counting on people believing all this. He chose this bar for a reason, and he takes a sip.

"What do you think?" Martin asks. "It's the new winter wheat."

"I'm tasting a little apple in it," Reynard says.

"You're the second person to say that," Martin says.

"And here I was trying to be original."

"I think it's just the honey, hitting the same place on the palate."

Reynard takes another sip. "I want to think about the palate all day. Let's trade jobs."

"Let's trade *debt*," Martin says, retreating a little.

"Hey, I know," Reynard says. "Let's both of us trade our problems with any two guys in Senegal."

"Amen to that," Martin says, and that bone thrown, Reynard quicksteps over to the jukebox. Jazz of the futurist variety, it offers silently, from 1979. A song that what's-her-name loved in high school. And there in the glass, the reflection like a photo framed by the doorway, is what he came here for.

"Hey, Rachel," Martin says.

Rachel Nickels, wife and mother, slopes into the bar saying hello. Reynard chooses a number and gets back to his seat. She comes here, there's nothing wrong with that, during a slice of unsupervised time Monday Wednesday Friday, when the babysitter collects Nicky from the Kitsune School and

Rachel's flexible workplace lets the radar lag. She could take over the snacks and the flashcards while the sitter keeps the laundry at bay, and she could sit in her makeshift home office, picking at electronic correspondence like rows of wooden ducks. She could run. She likes a gin and tonic, though. Martin's already mixing it up using a trick with a mortar and pestle that makes the drink taste, just a little, like rolling around in the woods. She sips and says, without looking at the man two stools over, "Well, this is awkward."

"I'm glad you said something first," Reynard says. "Do you—?"

He is gesturing to the seat between them. She shrugs a little, mid-sip, and he slides over, his jacket at his old place like shed skin. He's close to her now, for the first time since they recognized each other at morning drop-off. Rachel can hardly look at him, or take her eyes off him, and Martin, a possible lifeboat, bobs out of reach staring into his screen.

"I bet we're both thinking the same thing," Reynard murmurs. "That we're both, mother and preschool teacher, irresponsible to be here."

Rachel sips big. "I was thinking, that's the guy who wrecked my wedding." She says it loud enough to make the barman look up for a second at Reynard, peering a bit at the beard. But then Stanford knocks on the bar's open door. "Come out Martin, come out Martin," he says with unconvincing cheer. "Some bottles broke in the truck. Cabernet I think."

"What am I supposed to do?" Martin asks, although he's already grabbed towels.

"Bring fruit salad," Stanford says, ducking back out. "We can make sangria."

Martin doesn't say anything, and in some ways hasn't said anything for three foggy years. The weather has been bad, and so goes his life. He makes a lot of lists, and he tries to keep Gail Padgett Bottle's name off them, the way he shouldn't list finding a suitcase full of gold, or never again experiencing a hangover. There are fewer possibilities hanging around, and fewer customers too. It's not quite a failure, his life's work right here, but even thinking it's not quite a failure is more failure than he can really stand to think about, and every night he still stares hangdog at the window looking for her silhouette. He slumps across the bar like the towels are a ton of weight, and this premise, those solid bottles breaking to lure the barman out of the place, this reason Martin and Stanford are not also staring at Reynard in recognition—well, Reynard does not know if this is the action of a ghost or a bump in the road. He cannot always figure out what he can do, only what he wants. This may or may not make him marriage material. At least now, though, he is alone with this woman.

"That wasn't me," he says.

"I recognized you the second, the *second* I walked into the school. So don't."

"I mean I'm a different person," Reynard says. "That was, I'm very sorry about it, I should have started that way, straight out I should say how sorry I am, a very bad time for me."

"Don't worry about it," Rachel says.

"I mean it."

"OK."

"I was an addict then. I stopped all that. I'm a new man, a different person."

"I said OK."

"I cleaned up, I stopped drinking."

"You're having a beer," Rachel says, "*right now.*"

Reynard grins, *You caught me,* and makes a gesture with his hands that would go better with a cane and a straw hat. "A beer is as close as I can get to not drinking right now."

She can't help laughing, just a little, like the tip of a foot in the door. Reynard hopes he has kept his eyebrows from rising. "I know it doesn't look like it, sitting here like this, but I've reformed."

"Does the school know?"

"Are you going to turn me in?"

"So, *no,*" Rachel says, ice smacking her nose.

"They noticed a hole in my résumé," Reynard says.

"And you filled it with lies. I thought kicking drugs meant making a fearless inventory."

"I'm not *fearless,*" Reynard says. "Just sober, basically. Plus it wasn't that kind of program."

"How did you beat it? Hypnosis?"

"Spiritual practice," he says, and this being California, the answer doesn't get the scorn or even notice it perhaps deserves.

"*Nevertheless,*" Rachel says, "doesn't a reformed addict go around apologizing to the people he wronged?"

"I *am* sorry, sorry about it. I know I wrecked your wedding, the fight and the accident and all that."

Rachel puts her drink down, *slank,* as the accident comes back to her. "You went *missing.*"

"I was on a binge. I was *always* missing."

"But you turned up."

"Of course I did. And reformed. And sorry."

"It's OK. It's a story, really. We tell it to everybody when everybody's talking weddings."

"Like getting mugged. Terror becomes anecdote."

"I don't know about that," Rachel says seriously, "but *nevertheless*. Apology accepted."

"It really was the drugs and not me."

"Didn't you, you know, take the drugs?"

"Sorry, I can say again."

"I already said *accepted*."

"OK," Reynard says. And it is. The room loosens up enough, according to plan. "So," he says, "wrecky wedding, but you're still married?"

But Rachel's thoughts are broad and at liberty in the long tradition of the first drink's last sip. "How can you be sure," she says, "it was the drugs and not you? How do you know that your essence, your real whatever, the spirit of you—is the good, kind part? What if the addiction, the chemicals making you angry and violent, what if those are the real you, and the kindness is the imposter, the disease?"

She's quiet for the last five seconds of the song, long enough that Reynard thinks he's supposed to be answering. "Well—"

"Because, you know how they say with love, living with someone, how you can't believe that you love someone so much, and then sometimes you just want to pummel them with a big wooden plank and watch them break their legs down the stairs?"

"Sure, that sounds familiar."

"So what if it's like that? What if the awful part is actually the center of the marriage, and the intruder, the drug, is when you love them? What if *that's* the thing to try and get rid of, and the seething urge to, you know, drown them in the river, is really who you both are?"

Now there's no music, just a blank stuffy space where someone, Reynard thinks, should be talking. "That's kind of a complicated answer to the question 'Are you still married.'"

Rachel laughs and shrugs with the last of the drink. Reynard's beer has vanished too. This would be the time for another round if the barman were here. Instead—

"Are you that sad?" Reynard asks.

Rachel laughs as if to say no, but does not, does she, actually say the word. "Everything is just a little caved-in lately," she says. "Ben, that's my husband, he's moving up. They plucked him out of the management pool to work with the Vic on the Trail, some aspect of some part of it that always lasts late. It wasn't, you know, like how it was, how *he* was, when we first—I never see him now, and we *never* see each other."

"You have a beautiful little boy."

"Nicky is a *girl.*"

"Whoa, really?

"Yes, does everyone think—"

"I'm more with the other grouping," Reynard says.

"Grouping," Rachel says with a sigh.

"Groupings are part of the philosophy of the school," Reynard says, almost respectfully.

"I know, I know, Nicky's in Sweet Cookie. And you?"

"I'm with the Baby Jaguars."

Rachel groans. "That's so much cooler than Nicky's. *I* want to be in the Baby Jaguars. The whole philosophy, I can't follow it."

"Aren't you on the list? It goes out all the time. It's full of photos."

"I don't read it carefully. I scan for Nicky's little face and delete. I don't read *anything* carefully."

"What do you do?"

"I have a job they charitably let me pretend to do half-time. They're too nice to let me go, or afraid of a lawsuit, probably."

"What do you do when you're not working?"

"I make and eat pancakes for dinner. I wait for Ben. I come here for drinking drinks. Where is Martin?"

"Who's Martin?"

"The barman."

"So you come here often," Reynard says, as if he did not know, and looks at the cash she already has waiting on the counter.

"Monday Wednesday Friday."

"I'll join you sometimes, if I may."

"You stopped drinking."

"I spend eight to two thirty watching over children according to the methodology of Japanese folklore," Reynard says, in his defense.

Rachel is very much smiling at him, bewitched a little by this maybe-reformed man. He has not suggested a class, a therapist, a vitamin, an exercise routine daily, a book of verse appearing chapter by chapter on her phone, a *spiritual practice* even, instead of gin. Her heart is, just a very little, thumping in horse hoofbeats. She is restless, not scared. Not much.

"As the barman is missing," Reynard says, "I suggest we take a walk."

It's a faint line, but it's a line. You may sit in a bar, as a married person, alone. You may have drinks, and then it is natural to turn in conversation to your drinking neighbors, particularly if you recognize them. To walk, Rachel thinks, and instinctively they seem to be approaching the woods of the wedding site, is something else. It is not adultery, of course it isn't. In some cultures she would be stoned to death for such a thing, laughing openly with a man who is not her husband, no matter how reformed or good with children. She's not in that culture, though; she's in San Francisco, right at the entrance to Bottle Grove. He has not touched her, not even on the shoulder, or a little push. Those are amateur moves, Reynard knows, reckless, savage even. Too bold. He does not touch her because it is clear, the damp air on his face and flickering lips, that he will do so in the future.

Martin's missed them entirely. His eyes have time for nothing but the woman he's dragging into the bar. Padgett looks great, for the most part. Her hair is cut expensively, surely one of those places where they give you wine while you wait. She has not gained or lost significant weight over the last three years. She is wearing, Martin does not care what she is wearing, his hands so sweaty on both her shoulders now. Stanford comes in then almost at a gallop, his arms laden with purple wet towels. "Where were you?" he asks Martin. "Where did you go?"

"He saw me across the street," Padgett says, and Stanford sees her for the first time and drops the soaked towels in surprise. They fall like a corpse, *plop*, the ghastly sound of successful suicide.

"No, no, no," Stanford says to her. "Do you know what kind of work I've done on this man since you—no, absolutely not."

"I need everybody," Martin says to him, "out of the bar."

"*No*," Stanford says, like your mother says *and that's final*, but Martin glares him toward the door, both hands still on Padgett.

"He's a grown-up," she says, "we're all grown-ups," although it does not seem this is so. There is a wildness, is one way to put it, prominent right this second but usually kept fenced in. It growls beneath friendships and romances, loyalties and networks, underneath every society pretending it's working itself out. It is at odds with all careful talk and considerate action, thrumming and rustling always in favor of thrashing it out. It's impossible, inapplicable to say you can't fight it. It's like saying you can't grab the whole wide sky, like you can't clamber over the ocean or everyone who has died. There's nothing to fight; you can't fight it because you don't. It has set upon Martin like a devil or a ghost, and Stanford is gone out the door and the door is gone too, latched and locked so it's just another wall, and they fuck on the floor of the bar like animals, although Padgett cannot think of an animal who has ever made her come so hard. She screams with it, leaving Stanford faintly astonished on the sidewalk near the street. His hands are winey and he looks at the curb for a dropped napkin or some piece of trash clean enough to clean his hands. When he finds nothing, he strides across the street, the wires for the streetcars stretched over him like the trails of shooting stars.

Around the Blend is open, quite full. Paper napkins are in a basket with sugar and other sundries. Stanford wipes down and tosses them away. His hands are still sticky but oh well. He makes a vow, again but no less fervently and annoyed, that Padgett is not his problem, and tries diligently to believe this while he waits in line. He will order a coffee he does not need. Do not make enemies on the block where you do business, do not steal napkins and vanish into the evening dim. Martin will be a wreck anyway, with Padgett leaping upon them—Padgett who is not his problem—so Stanford should have energy for the work tonight while Martin sulks, broken.

He pulls out his phone and moves through correspondence as distraction. A party, a friend. A noble cause. People behind him in line, and ahead of him, are all rolling suitcases with their handles pulled straight up like lifeguard chairs. *What culture am I in?* Stanford wonders, now and often, about this adopted city that is raising him. He is getting older, less likely to be successful or even noticed, even if he keeps up with the weights. He sleeps around less, or at least less often, his twenties as gone as that cabernet, notes of berries and nonsense, that sliced him a little between his finger and opposable thumb.

"Large coffee," he says, when it's his turn.

"To go?"

"No, I'll drink it and leave."

"Because the large lids today," she says, frowning into a mug and choosing another, "we're not trusting them."

"I'm also," Stanford says, "having a crappy day at work."

Her associate, setting up the little paper cones they use at this place, nods along. He's a man with earrings that must be kidding, and he slides the mug under the apparatus with the practiced hand of the guillotiner. "Let's all run away," he says, "live on nuts and ferns."

"I don't want your nuts, man," Stanford says, and both coffee people nod like he's caught a ball. Some suitcaser clears his throat behind them, and Stanford wants to explain what he's taking refuge from, the crazies scheming and swapping spit in the faltering bar in which he's placed all hope that he could borrow or had lying around. But the second's over. He takes his coffee to the only seat he sees, at a square table that should not pass, in Stanford's opinion, for something you could share.

The woman opposite him is poking a message into her phone, which is flat on the table like it's prepped for surgery, her other hand gripped completely around her small beverage, her fingers so tight you can see her creepy bones. Her face is poached with worry and her long black hair hangs straight down like a final curtain, and in fact she will be arrested before too long for fraud, in the wake of a sex scandal. Right now she's trying to get her unreliable boyfriend to goddamn answer. Stanford only kind of notices her—she's been in the bar, maybe?—even with his eyes open. He is making a list, straight down a legal pad in his brain:

> *pitch more catering gigs, call Dawn again*
> *talk with the food truck guys again*
> *strike it rich, clear all debts, and purchase boyfriend*
> *no, marry money*
> *attack Padgett with ballpeen hammer*

and cannot believe this is his inventory. What could it mean, to have reached this place? He considers his own life the same way he, in his twenties, considered all the naked boys who woke up in his one-bedroom. Who is this? Was I the person doing such a thing? What does it mean, from the first people in Paradise such questions have we asked each other, me naked here?

Martin stands up from the floor of the bar and walks without a stitch on to get them both whiskey. Padgett's still on the ground of this rummy, almost terrible place, and he looks at her, sprawled naked like that, like a fantasy pasted up sloppily or an off-putting dream. Never a day has gone by but that he hasn't wondered where she was, those breasts and a pair of ribs angled oddly underneath her skin. What was publicly viewable, on the Trail and other networks, put her at seasonal openings and philanthropic gadabouts, but never here on the floor. His fingers chatter taking down the glasses; Martin's bones haven't been this jittery and sore since he threw over coffee.

"I can't be here long," she says, and he walks back to her. "I can't be here for a long time."

He pours long anyway and hands over the drink. She reaches up and takes it, and then with her other hand, holds him. His cock, limp now and wet, is folded up like a bat she stumbled upon once in the daytime, sick, she thinks, or just lost. He sips and watches her, her hand stretched up like that to his hairy legs.

"What are you doing?" he asks her.

She sits up, puts the drink down next to her. "I don't really drink anymore."

"Since when? I don't believe you."

"I've sort of phased it out."

He sits down cross-legged. Her hand is still around his cock. "Why," he asks, "would you do a thing like that? Your husband made you?"

"Kit's older now. She's harder to take care of hungover."

"Kit?"

"Kitsune. Our—the daughter."

"Right," he says. His drink's half gone and Martin watches Padgett look at the glass.

"I should go," she says.

"Will your Trail find you here? I guess of course it will."

Padgett shakes her head. "I left my whole purse and phone too many blocks away. Even my wallet, they can sight you through credit cards now, just a trial balloon."

"So you knew you were coming here."

"Yes."

"It wasn't just that I saw you from across the street."

"No, Martin. I was on my way."

She feels him thicken in her hands now, and at this she dreams for the first time of what her husband would say, what Vic would do if he saw such a thing. She takes her drink from the ground and sips it, then almost coughs around the whiskey, ashamed of her amateurism.

"So," he says, "sober, raising a girl, fundraising or what have you, I read."

"Are we catching up?"

"A lot's happened to you."

"Nothing *happened* to me," she says, and lets go of him. "I did all this. With your *blessing*, I might add."

"And today?" Martin says.

"I just had to," Padgett says, with another sip. "I was tired of thinking about you, without you around ever."

"It's just a little fuck on the side today," Martin can't help guessing aloud, now that his glass is empty, "off the Trail, or—"

"Don't do that," she says.

"I'm just asking. Three years, Padgett. You didn't even—"

"I called a few times."

"No."

"From weird phones. I *did*."

"I never—"

"I hung up when you answered."

Martin walks to the bar with half a hard-on. It is *exactly* like a dream, naked at work, and what is stranger is that Martin thinks he can remember at least one of those calls, a name, or no name, unrecognizable on his screen and then just a thin slice of ambient noise when he picked up, Padgett's attention like a lighthouse blinking through a roiling storm. "And what is it now?" he says. "Now you're going again?"

"I just wanted to see you," Padgett says. "I've been waiting to."

"Well, I'm like this," Martin says, waving a hand up and down his body like a quick tailor. "The same. And you, married to the Emperor of the Bay Area."

Padgett tilts to take another sip but her glass is empty too. Martin hands her his and goes to refill the other. He brings the bottle back with him. There's a scuttling at the door, someone pushing a little to get in and giving up immediately. Padgett looks at her expensive top on the floor, wadded. "I thought I'd feel togetherer than this," she tells him, "at least by now."

"It's hard, marrying for money."

Padgett gives him a look.

"You're *earning* it."

"Stop it, Martin. *Stop it.*"

"I'm just trying to figure things out," he says, throwing out his hands, and Padgett has to admit that the naked two of them, on a dirty red carpet with a bottle between them, is something that needs figuring. "We had a plot, a planned-out plot. You were going to marry this guy."

"I *did*."

"—and then in three years there's not a peep."

Padgett drinks. "Peep."

"Now *you* stop."

"He sees everything, Martin. He found the album. I had to stop posting at you, I don't know what he would have figured out."

"So what did you do?"

"I *married* him," Padgett says miserably.

"And what? Fell in love, you're going to say."

"No, I wasn't going to say that."

"Then it's according to plan?"

"It's a marriage, Martin. *Three years*."

"And?"

"And we make it work, I guess," she says.

"Aha," Martin says softly.

"There's no aha."

"You don't love him."

Martin watches her not deny it, although Padgett is just thinking that she hasn't said anything. It's unsettling how he looks at her, unsettling to both of them. "No one understands you," he says at last, "like I do."

"I don't want to be understood that way," says Padgett, and despite herself, pours them both more drink, falling down upon her throat like the shade of an umbrella. "I made a promise to him," she says.

"You are naked in front of me," Martin says, "when you say that."

She sips again and gestures to the sex they had. "I thought it was, I thought we could just—"

"Well, I made a promise too," Martin says, and Padgett almost covers her eyes in embarrassment. It is a speech coming, as sure as itch from a mosquito, or rain from a black cloud already raining, a speech made of whiskey and broke loneliness, a chip, for three years, on his weakening shoulder. "I promised I wouldn't let you slip away with everything, leaving me empty as hell. I set things, all of this, up. I rescued you from over a barrel, put on a party to throw you at him." He sips again while they both think over how far this is from what they both know is the truth. "You landed him and OK, you are making something work. When you go to a restaurant, you don't have to eat the food they bring out, even when you order it up and they serve it to you." His drink is not done but he pours more, and a little splashes to the floor. "But Padgett," he says, "Padgett, you have to *pay*."

Padgett watches it sink in, the whiskey, not far from her things on the carpet, her bra stretched out wiry and bent like a daddy longlegs. How dirty it is, where they are. She should put everything on and leave. "If it's money," she says finally.

"*If it's money.* Listen to you. Only a rich person, someone who could scatter thousands upon thousands—"

"Martin, I can't. The money's out of my reach."

"I just saw you *co-chairing*," he says, the word all wrong for his snarl, "an evening that raised one point five mil."

"And *what*? You think I can put a bunch of it in a sack and bring it to you?" She does not add "And that disease, that continent is *desperate*," because here he is, desperate too.

"How did you buy this shoe?" He looks ridiculous, naked, holding it up.

"On a card," she says. "The Vic's got the bug about cashless, you must know that."

"You see? You still call him—"

"For *you* I do. And for you I'd find money, but honey, there's nothing to be found."

The *honey* makes the barman clench his fists.

"I'm locked out of it," she says. "I'm out of the loop, I can have a Rembrandt delivered to my house in an hour probably"—she drains her glass and thinks for a second about whom she could actually call about that—"but I can't just fork something over to you. Vic doesn't even give up his money for his own projects—you need something of value to him to even get his affection. I mean, *attention*."

Martin pours more, almost too much for the tumblers to hold. It shivers at the surface, an evil lake. "That's it, then," he says. "That's what we'll have to do. Finish your drink."

"I've had more than I have in almost a year, almost," she says, hearing in her voice how she shouldn't drive home. This is her, maybe, she thinks, liquored up and in thrall to moody schemes. This is her with the marriage removed.

"Finish it," he insists, jumping into his jeans. "I will too."

So they do, and for a minute the bar is a volcano Padgett's in, the drink arsoning down her body. Martin too. He is scared, like seeing a horror movie twice, of what he knows he is about to say out loud.

"You're thinking something," Padgett says.

Martin empties the empty glass into his empty mouth again. "We could take her," he says.

Padgett brushes her hair, sloppily, uselessly, out of her eyes. "Take?" she says.

"You're the one who said, something valuable to him."

"But what do you mean, *take*?"

"Kidnap," he says.

Her first thought, over the thunder in her ears, is that she, Padgett, is kidnapped already, a naked prisoner on the floor, but that isn't possible, she lay down on the floor herself, she's an adult, isn't she? "What," she says, but now she knows it. "Who?"

"The daughter," Martin says. "Kit. The little baby. From that school."

"Have you lost—"

"*Everything*, I've lost. But this is easy. Do this easy thing, and then we're square as we ever were."

"*Square?* I've got to get dressed."

He puts one hand, sweaty with liquor, on her bare shoulder. "No."

"*No*," she agrees. "This is fucking *terror*, Martin. You want to hurt a little girl—"

He is shaking his head fast. "It's not real kidnapping," he says. "Not really. It's a con."

"Who? Who does it?"

"Under the table," Martin says. "Over in hours. I'll grab her and put her someplace—"

"Where?"

"I know where."

"And if this went wrong you what, bury her in the woods? What kind of person do you think I—"

"It's not anything terrible, or anything like that. It's a con, I told you. Not an honest kidnapping. Basically I pick her up

from school, you pick a good day. Right when you're drop-
ping her. You scream and go home frantic. Then you get a
phone call—"

"He'll trace it."

Martin blinks, then looks at something lying on the bar
like a dead person: a phone Rachel, or that guy with the scarf
maybe, left behind. "He'll trace it to someone else's phone,"
Martin says, pointing over at it. "A lost one. People leave them
here like shoes outside a mosque."

"You can't get into some stranger's phone."

"That's my problem. Yours is panicking to your husband.
And forty minutes later she's back in your arms, a close call.
I mean how much would he pay, how much could the Vic get
his hands on in an emergency, with no questions asked? I
mean, make a conservative estimate."

"Sure, let's be conservative now."

He looks wide at her. His shirt's on, and except for his bare
feet, and his plans to kidnap somebody, he looks like Martin
Icke. She thinks of him stacking glasses, scooping ice into a
bin, straightening the rubber flooring wet and sticky from the
ply of the trade. "We can do this," he says, "*inerrantly.*"

"People like us botch up lunch," she says. "We botch up
parallel parking. We botch up having friendships and fun."

"According to my calculations—"

"*Mis*calculations."

He shushes her, actually says *ssh*, and pulls her, naked, to her
feet. She is unsteady, drunk, and she hates it, a dark choky
loathing, Martin's leading her farther back in the bar. His
denim legs scratch up against her bare hips. She has never
liked this, being more undressed than the boy. She hates it,

going down the cold stairs. It's worse than fuck. It takes her, this blurry scared path, to a cage she suddenly re-remembers, in some locked-up warehouse hidden in plain view. Whatever happened with that? It's a story from her wasted days, drunk and high all the time, and here are just cardboard boxes, dusty heavy curtains sagging on the walls. Here's just an ashtray and a sofa she thinks used to be, hideous, in his apartment. She's probably fucked on it, she thinks, fucked and thrown up.

"We'll open my computer down here," he says. "Your kid can watch a movie and drink a Shirley Temple. By the time the fish finds the genie it'll be over and done with."

"No," she says.

"That's a promise," he says. "This is a very safe thing, Padgett. Nobody knows this place. You don't even know where we are."

"We're underneath Bottle Grove," she says. "The bottom of the bar, the speakeasy." An illegal room, she thinks.

"OK, yeah," Martin says, and puts a hand on a box to steady himself. It falls a little, and Padgett has a quiet desperate relief that this man, the barman she loves sometimes late lonely at night, is drunk too. Maybe that's all this is. "Yeah," he says again. "But you might not know."

"No," she says, but it just sounds like an echo.

"Don't say no," he says, begging, is he, or threatening her. His voice is too tired to tell, but she feels threatened, naked down here.

"Or?" she says, and it sounds like she has a choice. It's been one she keeps making, marrying the Vic, staying married to him, raising the child. So is this, the same kind of decision. You can follow the consequences like a thrown spool of thread, unraveling back through the dark maze. Or—and she's drunk now thinking this—you can get out of the room he's put you in.

If you say *yes*.

•

What did she say, what words did she decide, to get here? Rachel stands wondering, in a boxy house right where a gridded neighborhood suddenly loses its thread, about herself. Reynard has rented it, for the two-night minimum, and paid via screen. You never know with these places—it could go good or bad—but it's nice, mostly, furnished down to the towels and a corkscrew. The only things Reynard brought here were a shiraz blend and her, someone else's wife. Although she wasn't brought, was she? She stepped in here herself, after walking for weeks. It's been weeks and weeks, and the decision of whether to cheat on her husband, which she is doing, or about to do, weighs heavily on her. As does Reynard's hand, giving her wine in a glass that's not his, but to which, after paying, he is entitled.

"I don't know about this," she says.

"Neither do I," Reynard says, raising his glass. "Never in my life."

"You're lying," Rachel tells him. "You cheated at *my wedding*."

"Not on you," Reynard soothes. "Never on you." Like the wine, almost garish in her mouth, his line works whether you want it to or not. She is drunk with him, somehow, drunk on the attention he pays her and a want to undress his shabby clothes. For weeks they have just walked and drunk, flasks, beers, disposable cups and bottles, all brought or fetched by a reformed Reynard. They passed them back and forth, just talking. As long as they walked, nothing, Rachel kept promising some invisible listener, could really happen. Could it? It was just a little wilderness, the forest where she was married. Safe there, not even a kiss among the stumps. But today they have come to this new place, Reynard retrieving the key from a box that unlocks for a fee.

"I have a husband," she tells him, but it just sounds ordinary, like having a shirt.

"And how did you meet him?"

She sighs and sips, drops to the rented sofa. "We met a few times, actually, although he never remembered. We met at a bar, at a party, and I was flirty with an old friend of his."

Reynard sits opposite, on a chair, watchful as a chess champion. "Where's the friend now?"

"Dead," she says. Maybe if she makes the seduction lousy, then it won't work.

"Were you drunk?"

"At the party? Don't assume that." Rachel takes another sip and feels her lips, juicy, relent and grin at him. "But yes. And then, the second time, he was on a porch with his girlfriend. She had this little dog, there's another story about that, and it was peeing, out in the backyard where we were both invited for brunch. One of those scraggly yards in the Sunset where nothing grows, like a flying saucer landed and the crops all died. We talked for like ten minutes, and again he doesn't remember that."

"That's bad," Reynard tuts. "Men should remember."

"Then I *really* met him," she says. "My husband. I knew I was going to meet him. It was a fix-up only I knew about. That Something Dragon place on Balboa, with lazy Susans on every table. He'd just been dumped. It could have gone good or bad, but this time I was *ready*. I wasn't young, tipsy, stupid, dreamy—"

Reynard leans farther in. "Innocent, reckless, nervous."

"That time he remembered," she says, "because that time the time was right."

"We met before too," Reynard says, "but it's only now . . ."

He doesn't finish it, just kisses her, on her denim, between her legs, which are, Rachel notices in the mirror put up to make the room seem bigger, wide open for him. Ready. What else do you do in a house you have rented in the late after-noon? You can drink in a bar, you can walk anywhere. But they are here and here they are. "This is all part of my evil plan," Reynard says, his lips against her fleshy flesh. He's got her standing up, his hands on her shoulders as he laps at her neck, and then down the stuffy hallway to the comfortable bed, the top of the window almost even with the tips of the neighbors' trees, and the cotton clean and soft.

"I know it is," she says, when she hits the sheets.

Reynard stands over her and reaches down to unbutton, unbuckle, unsleeve her out of what she, today, decided to wear.

"I should get dressed," she says now.

"No, no, no," he keeps murmuring at her body.

She doesn't want to, but her legs, she can feel, are open again. His hand is there like a breeze on a sheet. Who could she be, that this is happening? At every step Rachel has thought, am I this person, is this me, object of high school scandal, bride in a forest, mother in a bar, naked with a man from her child's preschool? This is no stranger, raising her hips to him. Reynard sighs hungrily.

"No," she decides again. "I need to get dressed."

Her lover gives up for a second, sits cross-legged next to her with a nervy sigh. "Because—?" he says, like the teacher he sort of is.

"It's *wrong*."

"*Wrong*," he says back, like it's the name of a guy he sort of knows. "You don't want to do it."

"Look, I made promises to my husband."

"I was *there*," Reynard reminds her. "I was in *charge* of it. I *officiated*. It's a con, Rachel. He doesn't make you happy."

"You weren't a vicar and you're telling *me* it's a con?" she asks. "*Nevertheless*. I'm a wife."

"You don't know what you are," he says, too kindly for what's just come out of his crooked mouth. "You were a bride back then, but now you could be a fiancée again, someone's, and just not know it yet."

Rachel runs her hands through her hair as if to rid herself of, whatever they are, the words he is purring at her. He leans over to say it to her again.

"You're in love with me."

"No."

"You *are*. I can feel it." She scurries away a little, looks down the hall at her shoes. "You're falling for me," he says.

She stands up, but she does feel fallen. "It's a mess," she says, pulling something on. "I got stuck in something."

"Something's name is Ben Nickels," Reynard says. "He works for the Trail."

She can't say, she doesn't think she can say, that she hates what it sounds like when Reynard says her husband's name out loud, so she just shudders a little. She feels it like the first whiff that something's charred and ruined in the oven. Surely Reynard can smell it too. Look at him, lifting both hands for a second so they move brief quick wild around his face, both ears, both eyes, around the mouth, hear no evil, see no evil, and the other one. It's a speech she is about to give. "All my life," she says, "forever since I was little, I have felt like things are after me. Wild things, beastly creatures, at my heels. All right? You know? I've tried to keep them down. I got married so I wouldn't rattle alone in an apartment. I had this baby that came, whoosh like you wouldn't believe with the pain, out of this hairy body."

"You're not that hairy."

"And I thought," she says, "in the hospital, finally, this is it. I'll be out of the woods, I thought. But there's no out of it, is there? It's all woods, and I feel worse now doing this. So, sorry, I'm apologizing, and thank you and please leave me alone."

"You forgot to thank the Academy."

"Fuck you."

"This is your chance to do just that," he says, as filthy as it sounds.

"No. I have a *kid*."

"Your kid's not here, trust me."

"I don't," Rachel says, "trust you," before she knows it. It's definitely true. She thinks Reynard probably stole her phone that first afternoon at the bar, before that first walk in the woods. She has spent weeks making do with an old spare, surprised it still works, afraid to tell her husband she lost the latest model even though he'd be kind about it. You can't cheat with someone trustworthy. You can only rob a bank with a bank robber, only snatch a child with a person who would do such a thing. Reynard is that man, and she has to get out of here, leave the scene of the crime. "Stay away from me," she says, and mostly means it. "Stop coming after me. I can't have people coming after me."

Reynard points above him, above both of them. "This cloud," he says, "over you, this beast or whatever you want to name it, it's just unhappiness, is all that it is. You can get rid of it. I can help you, and if you let me do it, I promise it will all go away. I'll vanish. You'll never see me again."

This is the thing he has waited to say, the angel he wanted more, even than her in this bed. It's a con, she knows, but also it's true. All this pursuit, since the start, has been in service of something, not just this, in a rented bed: something else, something bigger, wilder. Every night, sleepless next to her husband, she cannot remember what color eyes this other man has, and when Reynard looks at her she still can't tell what they are. "What?" she asks him finally.

"Let me tell you a story," he soothes, but it is a strange one, not soothing at all by the time it is done. It is a wedding story, or at least it begins there, when the bride demands that a fox be roasted and served at the feast, and the vengeful spirit of the wronged mate flies into the bride's body and tricks her into suicide in the trees. It snatches bodies to this day, wrecking lives and loves, and it cannot be defeated, not really, never shamed or killed. Not in this town. It can only be bought off, and now, here in a stranger's house, Rachel Nickels knows she will pay. Her skin feels loud and wrong on her body, as Reynard's mouth offers a small smile, hardly a slit, his face aglow in the leaving day. So many creatures, she thinks, all in pursuit, yet still she runs, yet still they are bounding after her. "So," he asks, when the story is over, "how much money can you raise?"

CHAPTER 7

S AFE IN BED, Rachel blinks boltily at the open window. Her husband does not snore. He does not fart or smell or do anything that could irritate her and justify the evening's plan. But in fact his kindness, his ordinary consideration even while sleeping, is irritating enough, and she stands up. The clock says it's time. Ben doesn't turn over. He'll forgive her, she thinks, she hopes, she thinks she hopes.

There are two bags in the closet in her office, a room that every day is less of an office and more of a mess. Nicky's arrival pushed things like her wedding dress, and a small square bookcase full of an abandoned master's thesis on gender in Laos, into the room. Laos seems farther and farther off. When they have another kid, this room too will vanish along with, let's face it, Rachel's job.

In one bag are clothes she can change into quickly, and she quickly changes into them. Her shirt is her own, something she's owned forever that fits like thin skin. In the other bag is, conservatively, about ten thousand dollars in cash.

With technology in the shape it is now, it is more difficult for certain wives to get hold of the money. Ben pays all the bills through a system devoured recently by the Vic's ever-widening maw. Some money drifts into her account when she asks him, but the real money is (of course) imaginary and electronic, impossible to grasp because it's intangible, implausible to steal because it's just a wisp of a bookmark tucked into a screen. Even when she knows the code—her birthday, always—it's not discernible how typing it into the rectangle can get bills into her hand.

So she's emptied her old forgotten personal account and then, casually and stealthily, she pawned things, things she owned, at an actual pawnshop, the sort of underworld she thought she'd only see in movies about people's journeys to this sort of underworld. Everyone was polite, Chinese men and a few Russians, off in the Richmond near bakeries with dusty tiered cakes and narrow ramen restaurants with white ceramic cats, some good luck charm or ghost-warding talisman, waving at her in the windows. What she hocked were wedding gifts mostly, extravagances still boxed, flourishes from a bygone or dreamed-up era of lavish entertaining, showpiece vases and decanters like the necks of drained swans. Marriage used to be about money; nowadays, Rachel thinks, zipping up her hooded garment, what is it? Something else, and she sets out.

It's Sunday night, midnight, deserted everything. She walks with a paper bag full of money, the stupidest girl, isn't she, in the history of the world. Not even her older phone on her, in case Ben wakes, in case he tries to call. In minutes she'll be another mugging story told in bars, *Can you believe this moron?* carved on her tombstone. She shouldn't be here, no. People who say they've tried everything have tried at most four or five things. People who have looked all over the world for their one true love have likely spent just a few years dating in one metropolitan area. She's not desperate by the terms of desperate. She can raise ten thousand or so dollars, for instance, and she basically loves a man very successful in his wide-open field. It has been a thrill to cheat, to fall for a man who will likely cheat her out of a sackful of money tonight. Maybe this, and she remembers thinking the same thing, entering doubtfully the same forest some years earlier in the passenger seat of her mother's car, right behind the shaky Mexican catering van, will make her happy.

The path closes in around her, a canal of dark. He wouldn't meet on the avenue, he wouldn't get a drink first. So here she is, on time, she hopes, and should she call his name or not, is what she is wondering. The world rustles around her and there's a very big very sudden noise, her own scream at the hand on her shoulder.

"Mother*trucker*!"

"*Trucker?*" Reynard's voice is faint in the night, her scream still a lollygagging echo in the eucalyptus. His hand pulls back.

"I'm *trying*," she says, after a deep breath, "to stop swearing. Nicky's sharp enough to imitate it."

Reynard's chuckle is a little refuge from the shock, but why won't he step closer? Why isn't he holding her or at least taking her arm?

"Where are you?" he says, drink on his breath. She can smell it.

"Here," she says, reaching out an arm and brushing the buttons on his jacket, which rattle teethlike.

"Did you bring the money?"

"Yes."

"I don't mean to be rude, but how much—"

"Ten thousand dollars, a little more."

In many places in San Francisco this is not a lot of money. In Bottle Grove in the dark it still is. *Don't mean to be rude,* she thinks, and then wonders, as she has so many times in these woods, what is going to happen.

"OK," he says. "Just down here more."

"On the ground?" She stumbles a hand below her knees, some weed tickling at her knuckle.

"No, no. We're going to the field, I told you this. We will rid you of all trouble."

"How?"

"The same way I reformed and stopped drinking." His breath comes at her closer, the words near and definite. "*Spiritual practice.*"

"This is how you stopped drinking?" She is asking doubtfully but she can hear her question in the dark and knows it's not doubtful enough. Nobody stops drinking with a sack of money in a park. She wants a drink herself, out here, and like a magic trick Reynard's flask is thrust into her hand, too hard, moving past her arm to punch her a little in the stomach, and she stumbles over a root in the ground, or her own feet.

Reynard catches her. He catches the bag too, and it's gone from her hands. She hears it rustle as her feet right her and the flask slides onto her palm. She closes her hand around the drink and feels how really frightened she is. Her husband is sleeping unaware and her other hand is scared empty. "I would have *given* you money!" she cries out. "If you'd just *asked*! There's no need for this."

"What are you talking about?" Reynard asks. He is closer than she thought, calmer, but she cannot see one single thing now. "The money's here. I thought you were giving it to me. Have a drink."

She has a drink, and it's another punch in the stomach, the taste sweet but lined with something, the way blood tastes like metal. She coughs under it, hands it back into the black.

"Mothertrucking strong, eh?" Reynard says. "Awamori. Distilled from rice. The distributor's been making a fortune and I've been drinking it all night." His face leans right to her now, and for a second she feels a bit of unshaven chin rub against her. "Let's get on the same boat," he says.

"Page," she says, and then: "I'm frightened."

"Me too," Reynard tells her, but he doesn't say it like a frightened person.

"You swear this," she says, "this *spiritual practice* will—"

"It should," he says. "This is hallowed ground, supposedly."

Her mind frowns, spins a little. "It's a park."

"It's a wild place," Reynard says. "Unboundaried in a city that keeps building up more and more."

"I'm scared of getting attacked and you're talking," Rachel tries to figure, "about gentrification."

"No one's going to attack you."

"We're in a park, in the middle of—"

"I'm here to protect you."

She does not say, does not have to, that he's part of, not protection from, her howling, silent fear. He senses it like a dog. "Rachel," he says, and she hates his coaxy voice, "I'm not going to rape you. We love each other."

It is the worst thing, she can think of nothing chillier and more unspeakable, to hear in the dark.

He takes the flask and she swears she can feel his long sip go down his throat, like a mouse in a snake. And then the flask and the bag of money are both handed back to her. Her hands rustle around the money. It's just a paper shopping bag, from groceries she bought, and the money is not that heavy in it. But, of course, even in her thumpy fear is the suspicion, the knowledge that it's a con, the certainty, of course, that the money is gone and tricked away. He switched it out. She swigs. If she will finally be attacked, she will not goddamn be sober for it. It tastes brown as a pelt, the sugar stringing at her under the strength of it, like wide-open kissing a badger among, she looks up, the no stars.

"There are ghosts in the world," Reynard horrifyingly says, "or whatever you want to call them. Dybbuks and tricksters, imps and irritants. The things that bother us and chase after us, spirits that compel us to do things we wouldn't ever, unbelievable things we'd never do without a monkey on our backs."

"Oh God," Rachel says. "What are you going to do?"

"We're going to release them," Reynard says, his voice a little dramatic, intoning almost, not unlike the ceremony he performed. Her stomach tumults around under her skin, like something emerging from a swamp. "There's a legend about this place, an old story that when Bottle Grove was for immigrants—"

"What," Rachel says, hearing the sob in her voice just as the tears become evident on her cheeks, "are you? You told me this, I know this."

"You don't know the end," he says in the dark.

He's going to kill her. Nothing could be clearer. Rachel begins to run but is yanked back the second she starts, his

fingers cold on her wrist. "Stay here and finish it," he snarls.
"The ghost can be bought off and we'll all be free of it. A bribe.
Ten thousand dollars I hope is enough. It's what I've been
prowling around for, pawning watches and old wedding rings.
It's so hard to raise money in this town, if you're not one of
those creatures in tech."

"Oh God I do not know," Rachel says, heaving with
panic, "what are you talking about, what do you mean and
want from me—"

"*We stand here,*" Reynard says, a loud proclamation too
freaky to be anything but awful, "*and offer this sum—*"

"*Take the money, take the money,*" Rachel cries, but the bag
stays in her hands. Reynard shuts up in the dark like the plug
was yanked. Nobody, nothing, says anything. Rachel tries to
control her heavy, frantic breathing. Yoga, she should have
taken more of it. A class, sessions of something, a retreat,
anything, *anything* but drink. The flask is in her hand, she
realizes, and she throws it into the night. It doesn't make a
sound either, or maybe it's covered by her own desperate
noises. She sounds like she's whinnying, or it's some other
animal right close and then growling far away. No, it's traffic.
And clear as a bell she hears something toll one, some church
nobody in this city, not yet, has struck down and shut up. One
in the morning. Her feet move like toddlers on the grass. She
is puffing as she makes her way with the bag, her burning
breath in her throat in a way she remembers from the early
parts, before the pain blinded everything away, of giving birth.
Her baby girl, her screechy bossy adorable Nicola Nickels her
husband, bless him, let her name. She's learned her lesson, but
like everyone who says they've learned their lesson she couldn't
really say what it is, only that she's paid for it, and when she

reaches, finally, the avenue and the entrance to the forest, she
sees by the circle of streetlight that she's wrong. It's open wide
in her hands. The money is still in the bag.

•

Across town from anything interesting, nearing midnight,
Lillian Padgett Bottle, mother of Gail Padgett Bottle and
member in good standing of the board of directors of Bottle
Grove, orders a refill of decaffeinated coffee. Padgett twists
her napkin in her lap like a soft cotton noose. Her mother can
make a dinner as long as a toothache if the impulse strikes
her, or if there's a plan. Padgett does not know what it is. Even
in a very ambitious restaurant like this one, midnight on a
Sunday in San Francisco might as well be four in the morning.
The staff hates them both, and so does Padgett.

"I know you've heard all this, and I know you're tired of
it," Lil says. Padgett has narrowed her eyes to the width of
the last of the bottle of the wine they had with their torch-
seared urchin and their skittery greens with radish and their
whatever it was Padgett had—chicken, was it, something
from a farm. It is a bottle, right in front of her, that she has
promised herself not to finish, to ward off her mother's clucky
glares. Since the afternoon with Martin and all the whiskey,
sobriety has been a more difficult wagon, lunky and splintery,
no fun to climb back on. The world, it is plotting to give her
incidents and attitude that are violently, *desperately* thirst-
inducing, and the desire for another round, one more glass, is
a woodpecker's tap-taps on her sore skull. It wouldn't be good,
she knows. She knows something about wine, and that last

half glass is too warm to be good. It's too far gone, but she wants to get that far gone too, to catch up.

"You are a wife, Padgett."

Padgett can recite this story more easily than her times tables. A lot more easily, actually. Lil clatters her coffee cup down and mother and daughter, widow and wife, say it in unison as if comradely: "*The wife of a prominent man.*"

The waitstaff, in the corner where the espresso machine squats like a Buddha, reacts in Padgett's peripheral vision: *We're never going home.* "Do you know *how* prominent, Padgett? I don't think you do." She lays one hand over her other one and for a second Padgett has the faint hope her mother will wiggle them and pretend there's a turtle on the table. "*One syllable,*" Lil gasps or whispers, "is how he is known. Do you know this? They call him *the Vic*, one syllable."

"Two."

"Don't change the subject. I mean, do you, playing mother to that little girl—"

"Don't," Padgett says, but manages to just grab the water instead of Lil, "look at me like that."

"It's a look of, I was thinking, does she, my only daughter, know what she's doing?"

"Did you do this to my brother, too?"

"Don't say *did*. Matty's not dead."

"He's dead to me."

"You had a fight, is all."

"Six years ago. And he never calls me."

"He calls *me*, and says *you* never call *him*."

"And meanwhile he's still married to Her Awfulness, and he still makes money defending rapists."

"Alleged."

"It's not alleged, they're really married."

"Honey, your brother is a lawyer, that is the description of his job. He's successful. He's happy."

"So am I successful," Padgett says, mortified at her own hissing tone. She sees the server start toward her with water, and Padgett gives her the look of no thank you and the server gives her the look of OK but it's fucking midnight and could please you and your mother leave and Padgett snaps back with I know it's fucking midnight, oh God do I know it, and I am already planning to drastically overtip due to the fact that I am, as you very well fucking know, Mrs. Victor de Winter and the server gives a look, retreating, of OK I was just *saying*, and she's gone and Padgett misses her terribly.

"Of course you're successful," Lil is saying, like of course Padgett is a princess in a castle. "But you found him mourning his *wife*. You need the deal *sealed*, more than whatever hat trick you found—"

Padgett's mother tilts her head to look at her, and so, Padgett swears, does the bottle.

"What's *wrong* with you," Lil says, perking up. "Are you nauseous?"

"I'm not nauseous," Padgett says. "I just don't *care*, I mean *know*, what you're talking about."

Lil's eyes narrow like a fortune-teller's. "I'm talking," she says, "about your marriage. That little girl will be in his heart all day and all night."

"Actually, *all night*," Padgett says, "Kit sits in a chair that has a screen built *right into it* that's worth too much money, and laughs at *me* eating her sweet potatoes, because this month

Vic is closing some *loop*, and *all day* she's at a preschool which
operates under the principles of Japanese folklore."

"Have another one," Lil says, smiling very fiercely. She
sounds like a bartender, if only. "Have a real baby of your own.
You've landed him, but land him for *life*, a husband like that.
Whatever tricky charms you picked up will fade, but that
baby, *Daddy's* little girl, will never really belong to you. Every
time we meet, Gail, and you take the menu and order wine,
my heart just *aches* with worry."

Padgett leans forward as if at the long taut end of a leash.
Her napkin has vanished from her lap—maybe thrown—and
her hands are at her expensive little dress, flippant and stitched
with little stars or flourishes or whatever the fuck they are. "I
don't drink," she says, "*nearly* as much, hardly at all lately, or
fairly lately, and I happen to know a lot, I've learned a great
deal, about wine."

"Don't spin this at me, dear. I married into the Bottles
knowing they were all animals for liquor, your father included,
God rest his liver. He was the brass ring, with my grandfa-
ther's money turning to cardboard. All my life I was told this,
told exactly what to do. And I did it. Our house, the Padgett
house, would be long gone had I not schemed my schemes.
You think I loved him, Gail? All the time? I did what we
wanted, best I could. What we wanted was a boy and a girl,
Gail. What he wanted was *you*. And look at you now. You
think the world loves you fierce and independent, believe me
from the bottom of my years of experience, Gail, nobody does.
And all I'm trying to do is to *impart* a little—"

"You have no knowledge, *none*, of what you're talking
about."

"All the *knowledge* in the world," her mother says, the word *knowledge* rolling in her mouth like *cancer*, "won't make anything easier. Suffer less, Gail. Have his baby. Every night when you take your first sip"—and here Lil strong-arms across the table and empties the warm white wine into Padgett's glass all smudgy with her fiddling fingerprints—"I know you're not pregnant and it breaks your father's heart."

"He's *dead*," Padgett says, blocking too late her mother's tremulous pour. "This is crazymaking."

"Finish the wine while I finish the coffee."

"No, the wine's not what I mean."

"I tell you, you are making a mistake without another baby."

"We *just* got *married*."

"Three, what is it, years ago, you had no prospects and I was scrounging for you. Catering jobs. Without a kid of your own, his lawyers could throw you right back there like a snake."

"Nobody throws snakes," Padgett says. "I made some bad choices. Yes. I wish I could make them again. Also yes."

"You can't go back, but you can go forward," her mother says, with the triumphant use of something she saw tacked up someplace. Padgett's brain grinds around. She can't go anywhere listening to her mother, it's some difficult seat belt, her mother's hand crackling toward her, look, like it's made of wicked twigs. "Have a baby with him," she says, and her bright, bright eyes become, to Padgett, even nastier things to say. "Act like a real wife, Gail. Act like a mother."

If you want rage at its ragiest, tell a woman to have a child. Padgett stands up and lets her fury escape. Now it's everyone's problem. She looks around the empty place with the swivel of a tank, but it is only her mother in her sights.

"*Gail.* You're acting like—"

"You *make* me act like," Padgett sputters, "a *monster*, and the monster is *you*."

It's not, she can hear it herself, a good exit line, and neither is it a good exit. She's not drunk, because she's been careful, and so she has none of the bravado, the shiny self-image, that four pre-dinner drinks might have provided her. She's just thirsty, and she rages out thirstily, with her phone in hand already scanning for getaway cars. "We have an account, right?" she is yelling to the hostess at the door. "When we set up the reservation? Charge it there with a forty percent tip and escort the lady at my table off the roof of a skyscraper."

"You have to sign off on that," the woman deadpans, but then Padgett sees she is not, no she isn't, comrades-in-arms with her. She has the bill all set in a little leather thingy rectangle.

"Forty percent," Padgett insists, and hears herself, a snarling privileged woman getting a look of such truculent, such sneering superiority that Padgett misses her, misses all miserable servers, misses her own scornful life just a small handful of years ago, when she was just exactly this frowning exhausted employee with red zappy eyes probably full of cocaine, oh *how* she misses it, like a childhood dead dog, 100 percent.

But she's out. The night's all thick and starless, the neighborhood so quiet it looks carpet-bombed, the mannequins in boutique windows frozen up in morgue poses. Nothing, says the phone. Midnight on Sunday is too late, milady, but then there's an honest-to-goodness taxi, old-fashioned yellow, spurned in the world of clean smooth black professional vehicles her phone can summon in minutes. She stands in the middle of the street, feeling like a hooker, and flags it down with both hands, one clutching her phone and the other, *there it is*, holding the restaurant's napkin, which she drops into the gutter like a white flag.

"This isn't one of our hired competitors," the driver says smugly when she climbs in, and the music is too hip, too. "You have to tell me like a person where you want to go."

She spits out an address and gets slammed against the door when he turns sudden and rough, *good*. The night air looks bruised too, and out the window down a long street the streetlights all synch to red. When she was a kid, her mother said the lights were timed, and somehow she thought they sensed when the Padgett family were in a hurry and when they had time to stop. She was wrong about every speck of anything. The cab shakes through the city. They're putting up condos where five years ago Padgett would not have spat on the ground. "Hurry," she tells him.

"Ma'am," says the guy her own goddamn age, "I'm not in your hurry."

"You are," she says. "You're at the *helm* of it, and you know—" She bites it off, the phrase like cold scrambled eggs in her mouth, *who my husband is?* Her voice sounds like her mother's, so terrible, *Have a baby*, in this cab moving slow as a goddamn earthworm.

Martin is working his mortar and pestle when she hustles into the place. It's empty almost; the bar is dying out. Padgett crosses over and steadies herself on a barstool, a centuries-old terrible standby strategy, and nearly shoves against the woman at what was once her usual spot. Padgett is not drunk, she isn't. She is just there, staggering. Padgett knows she's been like this for years.

"Padgett," the barman says, with a quick glance at the other woman.

"Yes," she tells him.

Martin pours tonic, not calmly. "Yes," he says, "it's you? Or yes to the thing we were talking about, you know, the thing before?"

Padgett says nothing. She takes a stool and so does her purse. Her phone is in it; if the Vic checks she'll say, what will she say, you know Lil. Lil was on a tear. Bottle Grove, she insisted. The other woman, the only other customer, takes her drink and moves away, clutching a paper bag like she's guarding a puppy inside. Padgett watches it go, and her gaze slides up the woman's face until she thinks, yes, she recognizes her.

"Well?" Martin asks.

"Rachel," Padgett says. "Isn't it?"

Rachel, another mom at the Kitsune Preschool, turns around slowly, with a tight vacant face like she's a mummy.

"Padgett," Padgett says.

"Oh yes," Rachel says faintly.

"We know each other from *school*," Padgett explains pointedly to the barman.

"It's nice," Rachel says. "To. See you." She sounds like a hostage reading cue cards.

"You OK?" Padgett asks. "Bad night?"

The mom steps back away with her crinkly bag.

"I'll see you tomorrow," Padgett says, looking rabbit-panicky at Martin. "We can't talk with her here," she whispers.

"We wouldn't have had to," the barman says, and shrugs at her. "You promised you'd call me this week at the latest."

"I guess I had better things to do than keep promises," she says.

Martin is pouring two bottles, one in each hand. To Padgett it doesn't look like enough. "But? So? Yes?"

"Words of more syllables," she says, "and make it a double."

The whiskey, clouded with some other ingredient, appears like a topaz in front of her. He spoons in something else, lighter, that floats on top and then ghosts on down. "Rye and lemon," the barman says, "and then I add the Benedictine last minute. Frisco Sour."

"I'm sour on Frisco myself."

Martin leans in to her. "We could do it tomorrow," he says. It looks theatrical, the lean, overly conspiratorial in a bar with just one other person in it. But it is a conspiracy, is something she is trying not to admit. Padgett doesn't say anything back, but it's hard to tell how Martin takes it. "I was about to message you," he says.

"The threat of a message," Padgett says, like a narrator, and Martin's eyes flash.

"The threat of the Vic reading it," he says, tossing something too hard to the sink. "The threat of the Trail. The threat of fraud uncovered, and divorce."

The word, spoken out loud, is a rattler in the room. Padgett wants to hiss back but her palms are too freezing cold.

"I deserve this," Martin says. "Money's my last chance, Padgett. I have nothing else I can stand on."

"Nothing," Padgett says, "but a little child."

"An heiress," he corrects.

"If you hurt her—"

"Hurt her," Martin repeats in easy scorn, but then says, "Don't get panicky," and smiles like it's almost normal. "This is a nonviolent, one-man job."

"*Person*," Padgett says. "And there's no such thing. It takes you two guys to run a bar."

"Stanford's off tonight," Martin says. "It's not his job. It'll be me picking up Kitsune tomorrow, right when you go. I know the route."

They're hushed now, and Padgett gives Rachel a tiny glance. Padgett grasps the glass; it's superhuman of her, she should get a medal, for not having sipped it.

"I'll bring her here," Martin says quietly. "She's easygoing, you always tell me."

"I do?"

"You do. You told me, you told her you're not the actual mom and it was water off her back."

"It was."

"And then I'll call the Vic. I have a phone and everything."

And everything, it sounds like elementary school. Padgett gazes into the whiskey crystal ball trying for answers. She tries and tries and it refuses her. "And what will you say?"

He lifts her drink and sips it. "A little small talk," he says, "and then, if you want to see your little girl alive again."

"Are you really going to do this?"

"*We* are."

"You are making me act like a monster," Padgett says, "but *you're* the monster," and it doesn't work this time, either.

"You can hate me, I guess," Martin says. "That's a good sound philosophical position. But we're in the thick of it. Do this with me, and we'll be out of the woods."

He is promising something. His face is afire with it. She cannot help, tenderness so recent between them, but believe, not what he says, but nonetheless believe *something*, an outline where they've traveled together, a tamped-down trail they share. "I don't hate you," Padgett admits, "but that can be a placeholder. You're talking about a *crime*."

"We're talking about *money*, and conning it out of someone," Martin says, "and what's the matter with your drink?"

She looks at it. She looks the whole thing over. Nothing, she guesses, and says nothing as she drains it. Nevertheless, it seals the deal. A large grin, eagerly curvy, moves from Martin's forehead to his open face, as if this were the parade he has been dreaming of, this whole time she's known him. "Last call," he calls at last, happily.

"One more," Rachel says, returning with the empty glass and the paper bag. She's been at the jukebox but hasn't even chosen a song. "One more before I go home to my husband."

Her husband. Padgett tries to track it out, this married life people get themselves into. It's something she'll never comprehend; every grip she has fades into the gauzy night like a paper doll in water. She is moving her fingers on her phone, to get home to her husband and his precious child. She is married and drunk, a mom and a criminal. She is leaving and she is stuck here, nowhere near out of it. It is all, wherever she looks as the phone searches the night, the whole world is the woods.

●

It's dark everywhere. Rachel lets herself in and puts the bag down. Her office is spooky this late. She can smell the whole night on her, forest and fear, gin and tonic, that other wife, Padgett, muttering in the bar while her heart terrible thumped. She wants it all off her. She strips there and stands naked in the hall, peeking first at Nicky and then at her husband, still silent in bed. Her guilt, her loss is a beesting, forever lodged it feels. She is hunched and cold, her arms goose-pimpled and her breasts shrunken like the sea-wrecked last of a sandcastle. She showers in the off-putting splendor of scented soap, crying a little. She thinks of Reynard vanished—*bought off*, is how he put it, but he didn't take the money, just disappeared into a dark so dark it felt like everything had disappeared already. Where are you, where did you go, she is thinking, about the vanished man or herself. It feels like she is even asking the innocent man she married, waiting dreaming in the bed.

The shower doesn't wake anyone. Rachel wraps herself up and, before slipping into the dark bedroom, takes one track-covering look at her office. The bag looks wrong, and when she opens it, dripping, it's true. By the late light she can see the money is absolutely gone. She looks around the room, the lay of the land, and back inside the paper bag, creased and translucent like new skin. She asks it again, she will keep asking.

Where are you, where did you go.

CHAPTER 8

THE KITSUNE PRESCHOOL of San Francisco's ad campaign—*Kitsune School Makes Me Feel Famous*—features a photograph of a girl of indiscernible cultural fingerprint: a citizen of the world. It is run according to the principles of Japanese folklore, its hand-drawn mascot the nine-tailed fox. The school is about to be made famous for shutting its doors, and the fox's story is also one of transformation—indeed, the tale drifted into Japan from Chinese storytelling, and before that who knows—about a creature who lives for hundreds of years, in one treacherous form or another. She begins as a courtesan, which is, at the school, underplayed, but is hero and thief, lover and rival, murderer and tree, over the wild courses of the story. The fox disappears and reforms, pounces and changes costume, and similarly every day at the Kitsune Preschool is a new one. Circle Time is at the beginning or the end of the day. Different groupings are encouraged to start and disperse. One student may lead a song and the next day sit in back, and there is snack or there isn't or there are two snacks. The idea championed by Maureen de Winter, until her shocking death, is that the new generation learns to be a part of constant change, in the current world with technology ascendant and important and mercurial and fun. The story of life keeps changing, so once you decide what sort of story it is, you have locked yourself into thinking unhealthily. Ill-behavers are forgiven almost before they're done misdemeanoring, and the furniture is moved around daily, except when it's not. The philosophy of change and reformation extends to the hiring of its staff, which includes among longtime experimental enthusiasts and other young women an ex-con, a reformed felon. The head of the school, Ariel, hired him for his openness and honesty and willingness to change, and because she was sleeping with him. She is not a felon herself, because she has not been caught, but a few years back, she took some of the money meant for the school and saved it for herself, in case of a rainy day, betraying legally and morally her old college roommate. She would likely have been caught had Maureen not died. Ariel thinks this for the millionth time, in a bus station, panicked and soon to be trailed and caught. She's kept the money, but the felonious spirit has moved on to someone else.

Martin's running late, the Mission traffic thick in front of his van and the sky above scowling dark. It is not raining but it looks like a rainy day. He knows how to get to the school, knows it cold, but is having trouble backpedaling in his head to how he's here. His screen won't do that for him; it's a story he has to tell himself. One night a girl appeared in a forest in an apron and stole a barrel. He, Martin Icke, walked with her out of the woods and then for several years more or less died. Now they are doing something together. It is a risky idea, a bad idea even. But it is *theirs*, together.

The van's radio manages music for every mood or occasion, but Martin can't figure out what to listen to on the way to a kidnapping. Dance songs about dancing keep his mind on the moves. He has Rachel's phone, left behind at the bar, that opens up to her birthday, which he took note of some time ago. That was smart of him, he tells himself, and now the phone is shiny in his pocket waiting for instructions. He feels it there like a charm, ready to call the Vic and summon up money without ever tracing it to him. Martin is gambling his entire life on Padgett. She is gambling hers on the Vic. They'd better, he tells himself, win.

Padgett's at the place where she and Kit always split a bagel, splitting a bagel. San Francisco's bagels are wretched and spongy, but nothing would sit right in Padgett's stomach anyway. She tells herself it will help her performance, these butterflies, aid in her transformation into the panicked mother of a snatched child.

"Bagels make my hands sticky," Kit says.

"We don't have to worry about that," Padgett soothes. "Because of . . . ?"

"Napkins," Kitsune says.

"Which start with the letter . . . ?"

The little girl thinks, thoughtfully. "*W.*"

"*W* is just your favorite letter to say, silly," Padgett says, crossing the street unnecessarily. They drew it on a paper napkin, the quieter sidewalk, the driver's door. By the hydrant, if it hasn't happened yet, she will stop and fuss over the child's buttery hands. Butter is what Kit will remember, Padgett thinks, she hopes, the only thing from this day.

"Second best is *X,*" Kitsune says, having chewed this over with the bagel. Padgett grins back at her and kisses the apple-smelling top of her head. She's a quick little girl, the kind, Padgett thinks, who will learn everything, bright-eyed facts and methods of which Padgett did not, and will never, dream. School for Padgett was just some shoe she put on each morning, a dead building she walked into without more than a glance. She never really wanted to learn anything, and by God she hasn't. The future spreads out from each moment, right now, like passengers in the water of a shipwreck, struggling every which direction. This scheme will be a blip, failure or some skewed success, Martin in prison or out from under debt, the bar a San Francisco landmark or another floundering room. Kit surely will be safe—it is unthinkable to think otherwise, these little fingers shiny and grubby, resistant to Padgett's mouth-moistened napkin—and she herself, what? In trouble too, betrayed and betrayer, or somehow free and clear. She thinks of the parade Martin wants, music and floats and what did he say, confetti. Happy and ruined, desperate and triumphant, like snowflakes all these routes seem finally the same.

Her phone doorbells while she's at Kit's face, and then doorbells again. "Two people are calling," Kit says.

"I know," Padgett says brightly.

"I want a phone."

"When you're six," Padgett soothes, but it's too late now, or at least almost. Padgett's phone is on time—it must be, nothing runs fast or slow anymore—but the school, across the block, doesn't look early. Normally now the entrance is quiet, but she can see parental figures, the preschoolers holding their hands like scarves dangling. They're in little groups, worrying together or just chatting, as pigeons do, and Padgett turns from them to her screen as it tolls again.

"Three people!" Kit says in delight. "One two three!"

"One two three," Padgett repeats absently. The messages, all of them, say call now. One is a mom she can't stand, toothy and full of drama, and then Vic and then Nina, whose tall body she can spot over there by the school. Cancellation, maybe? Something flooded, a fire drill? Will this plan come to nothing and Martin will do what, in panic or in fury? Is she relieved, is it time yet to be relieved? Padgett does not wait for an answer.

"You're pulling me too hard!" Kit says. "Padgie! You're pulling me too hard!"

"We're in a hurry now," Padgett says. She shakes her head like her whole morning, her whole lifetime, has gotten stuck in her eyes. "We're hurrying. One two three four."

They jaywalk—Kit is gasping at the scandal of it—with the street stretching out beneath her, it feels, like a frothing river, and Nina spots her and breaks off. Padgett makes herself not snap her head around to look for a van. There's something off in the air, smoke from a fire or maybe that new Thai place, or just the same fear in her throat and the palm of her hand, pressed up against the little girl's. Hurrying along next to Nina is a man, thuggish and stocky as a bodyguard, whom Padgett takes a minute to recognize as Gabriel, the husband who since a year ago does something-something systemizing with the Vic. It's made him rich, richer even than before, and he is puffing now in a coat Nina had made for him in Rome.

"Where's Daisy?" Kit asks. They're right in front of the school. "Daisy!"

"Go to her, Kit," Nina says, her eyes lightbulbed with panic. Her girl Daisy has the same shoes, which counts for friendship at their age. Kit lets go and scurries. Nina takes Padgett's hand, a big ring poking at her. "It's awful," she says right away.

"What is?" Padgett asks. Nina's face is so grim Padgett thinks for a minute the kidnapping has been pulled off, but Kitsune is *right there*, pigtailed and authoritative with her father's chin. Beyond her is the door of the school, chained and padlocked, the metal so ridiculously thick and clangy it's like an old cartoon. Padgett sees the shades drawn, shades she's never seen, sternly all the way down the big fingerprinted windows.

"Closed," Gabriel says, "for the duration, until further notice."

"Further?" Padgett says. "Notice of what?"

"Vic didn't tell you," Nina says.

Padgett's phone is all bells now, rung with the regularity of dance music, the kind drugs make better. They're all, most of them, from her husband. "I think he's finding out," she says. "He went in early today, to talk to New York when it opened."

Nina and Gabriel share a glance, the language of a marriage they've made work. Gabriel reaches up absently to fiddle with the ear stud Nina thinks is sexy. "There have been accusations," he says.

"And *only* accusations," Nina reminds them both, her tone indicating, of course, that the accusations are true.

"Sexual improprieties," Gabriel says, "with a staff member and a student."

"*Between* them," Nina says. "And don't say *student*, like it's some coed. A *child*. A child was attacked."

Padgett gives up on her phone. "What?"

"Right here is where," Nina says. "Kitsune School. That guy with the who-knows-why colored contacts who looks like my old boyfriend kind of."

"Reynard?" Padgett draws a police sketch in her mind, tosses it out. "No he doesn't."

"A *little*. Without the beard."

"He has a beard?"

"Sometimes. But Padgett, he was with the Baby Jaguars. That's your girl. That's Kit."

"What's going on? Where's Ariel?"

"*Gone*," the two parents, the spouses, say in unison.

"She shut the school and took off," Nina says, "as soon as it came in this morning. Nobody knows where she is, or the guy, that *monster*, or what is going on."

At *monster*, Padgett is half-remembering a story, long ago from Nina, a man with an animal face and the rest—*meat?*—lost in wine. "What *is* going on?" Padgett asks, and her feet seem to be sliding suddenly, like a beginner ice-skating, and when she grabs the head of a parking meter, cold and solid, she realizes she's grabbed it for support.

"Take your phone and scroll it up," Nina says, and Gabriel makes a gesture to calm her. "Thank God and nothing personal, Padgett, that our Daisy is in Yummy Cookie."

"Sweet Candy," Padgett says dumbly.

"Ariel sent out a message at seven twenty this morning," Gabriel says, like the lawyer he maybe also is. "In the wake of accusations the school is closed until further notice. The accounts are gone too. Call Vic, Padgett. His people have hacked in. They're using the Trail. They're trailing her now."

Padgett's feet keep sliding. Repurposed linen slippers, designed by the sister of another wife, do not help. No, this will not do at all, what is happening. She needs help, a drink or some other medical attention.

"You look pale," Nina says, and then shrieks her head back. "*Doctor!*"

"Nina," Gabriel says.

"There are nine top-class doctors with kids here if there's one," Nina says. "*Doctor!*"

"Let's all get ahold of ourselves until we know exactly what it is that has transpired." Gabriel is looking at his phone too. "I'm going to go. I will call you. I'll call *everybody*, later. Stick together. Take the kids for eggs."

"She's already had a bagel," Padgett says, "and I don't need a doctor."

"I should think not," Gabriel says, and puts a hand on her shoulder. Some night, at some drinks function, the two of them will be alone and only then, not here not now and not all the other times he has leaned in to Padgett like this, will they discuss their long-ago drunk flirtation in the speakeasy space. "It's just a shock. We need to disperse and take our children home and answers will come soon."

"But you," Padgett says, "you think it's true?"

Gabriel gestures to the chained door as though, for his next trick, he will step into a locked-up-tight building and emerge with the ace of spades. "You're a typical person," he tells her. "What do you think, with Ariel shutting it down immediately like this? Sexual accusations, unspeakable, and then the door locked? Once you see what kind of story it is—"

"What are you doing here?" Nina says suddenly. She is looking past Padgett, and Padgett turns around to see her scruffy secret, with bags under his eyes and his hands in his pockets. He is sort of grinning, sort of relieved, wary too.

"Martin," Padgett pretends to have retrieved from an address book in her head. She turns to Nina. "Martin Icke. From Bottle Grove."

"Hello," Martin says.

"Oh yes," Nina lies, and Gabriel squints at him.

"You'll have to excuse us, Martin," Padgett says, impressed with her own airy tone. "Something has come up."

Martin steps forward and back, a dance in Gabriel's lawyerly gaze. "Come up?"

"Martin and I were going to talk drinks for the fundraiser," Padgett says, concocting like an alchemist.

"Well, there's no fundraiser now," Gabriel says, disgusted, his thumbs busy on his little pad.

"We've just received," Padgett says to Martin, looking as closely as she dares at him, "some bad news."

"Bad news," he says, and moves his shoulders in a shrug or something.

"I'll have to talk to you later," she tells him. "When we get this all sorted."

The word in the air is "sordid." Martin has reached into his pocket and retrieved a machine Padgett hardly recognizes, an old, old phone. "You have my info?" he asks.

"I should, yes."

Nina somehow has heard something in this, some thread she ought to tug. "You were meeting here? So early?"

But Martin is already walking backward, half-turning around like there's nothing, and there isn't, to see here. "I had nothing else to do," he says, and Padgett, where does it come from, loves him a little for the last time. He goes, keeps walking, around the corner, a tall glass of water, a whole bottle, she thinks, of white wine down her throat, as soon as they get home. She never calls.

•

"We dodged a bullet," the Vic says. He's cupping his hand over his phone, a gesture so twentieth century it's jarring on her futurist husband. "Talk to you in a minute. Is Kit OK?"

"She's fine," Padgett says, but Kitsune has already hurried past. Now she stops mid-flight, in the bright kitchen, looking at her father in slack astonishment. The Vic holds both arms out like he's being searched at the airport.

"Daddy's working at home today," he says, his attention fierce on the phone.

Kit stares at him like a frog walked in. The world is so strange this morning. "You can't *work*," she says, with crazy-eyed incredulousness, "at *home*."

"How about a movie?" he says. "How about the V4U?"

"V4U!" Kitsune is doubly astonished, at her father and at her luck. She bounds into a room that once had no purpose and now is where Kitsune lies on her back, barefoot, and holds a tray-sized screen over her, embedded with a proto-type the Vic brought home like a conquering hero, V4U a working name for a system of things to watch. Padgett finds the name robotic and sort of sleazy, also the feeling she gets from Kit's eyes when she gazes at it. They are both watching her go.

"Do you know," the Vic says, "how many times I tried you?"

Padgett's body has been rabbit-thumping for so long she's forgotten how it used to feel, a normal rib cage and fingers that just stay there. "My phone was being an idiot," she says, "and *Vic*, the chains on the door, Nina hysterical, all the gossip, Kit asking questions, I just wanted to get home."

The Vic nods like that's fair enough. Kitsune is already giggling in the room. Another baby, is what the room, Padgett just figures out, is really for. "We can call Teresa, or who's the other nanny."

He means Tessa. Teresa doesn't work for them anymore. "I'm fine," she says. "I'll take her. Me and V4U."

"You sure? Did you have something today?"

"I was going to make," Padgett says, "some panicked phone calls."

Her husband's face sets. How easily the truth slides in, like a bookmark. "We dodged a bullet," he says again.

Padgett feels like the bullet is still hovering, though. "You think it's true."

"I think Ariel hired a creep, yes," the Vic says, although his eyes are sliding away from her. "And she was always one, too. She was conning Maureen all the time, telling her everything she thought she wanted to hear."

"What do you mean?"

"Padgett, I don't have time." He uncovers the phone. "She lied to Maureen. Took too much money. There's a lot of gears here and I'm shutting them down, but I have to *move* and I have to *move things*. Wednesday was supposed to be my Friday."

Padgett's purse has overturned. Things are clattering, all kinds of things, and it's tears, the way things are going, on her face. "I'm just glad," she says, "Kitsune's OK."

The Vic hangs up his phone. His arms are around her, all around her like she's hiding in them. She is. She is really crying but also, isn't she, a scam and a con. "Nothing happened to Kitsune," he tells her.

"OK."

"I'm telling you. He's a creep but it's probably hysteria. And I know what kid."

"I don't want to know," she says, because shouldn't she? And doesn't she? She has to remind herself that this thing, scandal or crime that locked up the school, is not her cloak and her dagger, not the scheme of which she was, and is no longer, a part. There was another story, bigger but harder to see, under her whole scheme, like love, or something else, under every moment of a marriage. She pushes her way out of him. He is looking at her and then at the phone. Her husband, she knows, is moving heaven and earth, and like so many wives, she is a bit player in a crisis, of little more use than a screen for the kid. It sickens her, it relieves her, to be far from her husband's inner workings, the corridors and trails of his power. Otherwise he'd know. He'd know it and he'd throw her down the stairs.

"OK," he says. "You OK?"

"Me OK," she cavemans back, with a little smile. "It's hormones, partially, it's possible."

He just blinks, so she wades farther in.

"I might be pregnant," she says, and that story, *might be*, is true as anything. She watches her status, her esteem, rise. With a baby she's a star. The Vic's eyes widen. The Vic's fingers cross with one hand. And with the other, while Kitsune laughs again, he is already calling someone back.

The movie is *Fox's Honeymoon*, a Kitsune favorite. It's of
Japanese origin and animated, just like her, although the
source material is Native American, as near as anyone can
tell. The network, voice-activated, found it when she uttered
her name: A fox loves a young man, and when he takes a
wife—the birds sing the happy couple a song that Kitsune
drones to herself in tuneless looped fragments while her
hair gets combed—the fox hatches plan after plan, pleads
for wish after wish from the magic waterfall. But the happy
couple journey on, married and settled, no matter what
tricks the fox plays, and at the end the fox has learned her
lesson and—Padgett never gets this part—fallen in love with
a snail. The erotic hush, unmentioned but omnipresent in
the blue twilight of the film, is something Kitsune will carry
with her, always and forgotten. It'll be part of her love life,
Padgett thinks, listening to the dim and plinky soundtrack,
and this is what the story is. You meet people and you tell
them stories. You meet someone, you marry them, and they're
not part of the story you're in. They are it. You're the same
story and as it changes, every living day, you can never, never
keep up.

•

"Let's keep watching," Ben says gently. "That's enough
checking on her, I think. Yes?"

Rachel has come back into the living room. The blanket
she's sharing with her husband has been pulled to the floor,
like shed skin, so Ben could go busy himself in the kitchen.

"She's asleep," Rachel admits.

"She's *been* asleep," Ben says, and she can hear he's making them drinks. On the little tables at either end of the sofa are the last knifed continents of pancakes, sitting in syrup like a sticky map of the world. They haven't had breakfast for dinner for ages. "I don't think anything happened."

Rachel sits down in her warmed spot. The screen sits paused at the edge of the blanket. It's a V4U prototype, one of two in circulation. It's just another screen with a choice of watchables, but it is testament to how high Ben has risen in the company that he gets the second one. In two years they'll have another baby, and a much, much bigger house. Their rugs won't be big enough; they'll look like towels, skimpy and replaceable, on a beach of hardwood floors. "*Nevertheless*," she says.

"I know there's reason to be worried but there's nothing, I swear, to be worried about."

Rachel looks at the blanket, frozen mid-wrinkle like a glacier. "How can you be sure?" she asks him.

"Because," Ben says, and sighs and works the shaker, trembles it all up until everything is cold, "I know which kid it is."

"Who? No, I don't want to know. But if he," and she stops. It's just something to say here. An ax has fallen into the middle of her life. It is powerful but it's left just the tiniest of marks. She knows Reynard was not inappropriate with her child. He was inappropriate with *her*.

"I think the whole thing was nothing," Ben says. "The Vic was on it—"

"I can't believe you still call him that."

"He was on it all day. Something with his wife—the dead one, the first one—and money from some accounting scheme.

Ariel, she's the real criminal, that's the real story. That guy Reynard was just a sleaze. The Vic took care of him."

It's the *was* that pings in the room, like a bulb burnt out. "Surely the Vic didn't," Rachel says, but she can't, again, say anything more. Reynard in some shallow grave, stretched out just inches below the grass and the leaves, is something she can conjure up easily. It looks just like him in that rented bed. Ben brings in the drinks crackling with ice in the glasses they hardly use. He is trying very hard, she can see, to make a special evening after a bad day, and she does need a drink.

"You'll never see him again," he tells her. "Hide nor hair. Cheers."

"Cheers."

"Restart," Ben says, as the liquor greets her tongue. It's flowery at first, but that's just a soft glove over the punch of the tequila. It's a version of their wedding drink, she realizes, tequila and rosewater and lime, not as fancy as the original but still delicious and special. It's called something, but at Restart the movie chases away the name of the thing. V4U is voice-controlled, one of its selling points, a network of film and television that gets smarter, or not smarter but more familiar, more like you, the more you talk and converse at it. A young child's demands, Ben repeated from the meeting where they gave it to him, for the same thing over and over, or for something dreamed up entirely, can be granted in seconds, gratifying parents and silencing homes so wondrously there's half-joking talk of renaming it Deus Ex Machina. Rachel and Ben haven't shown it to Nicky. They've only shown it to themselves, to each other, indulging in the movies that brought them, with hilarious dialogue and plots so slow there's plenty of time for kissing, to courtship years ago. It's a grandiose vampire movie tonight, in lurid color and music, and it's been paused at the moment when the innkeeper has just found rice in their luggage and realizes our heroes are honeymooners.

The plot moves forward lugubriously, slowed down by bodices and moody piano playing. Rachel keeps sipping. The innkeeper's wife is hiding something, little items that make her cry when she opens the cupboard, and Ben thinks, darkly and fleetingly, of his own shoved-away stash. He'd stopped by Bottle Grove some time ago and asked for the recipe for the cocktail Martin had cooked up at their wedding. It was a pretext to check up on his wife. Her Trail kept stalling at the bar, like a footprint in the snow, the tracks of an idea that his wife's wanderings were actually, materially, unfaithful. Walking home he saw them walking, his own wife and his kid's own toothy teacher, and Ben found a new ruthless streak, fed by his rise in the court of the Vic. He made the call, conned up a crime. He said it as clearly as he could, that Reynard had assaulted his daughter.

Ben was willing to use his child this way, as lure and rumor object, to trick his wife back home. Now the man's gone, his rival; the school is closed, and the evidence, about ten thousand dollars, is zipped up and hidden away. It skulks like a cage in a basement, terrible but largely forgotten, as if it were just something he was told years ago, something he heard just once. Rachel's feet bump up against him under the blanket, and by the time the vampire has the bride in thrall, the drinks are empty and the prattling movie tossed away as the couple laugh and undress on the floor. He would not, will not let her go. Ben has connived, as adulterers connive; he will keep her, and the secret too. He has to con her, a little, that he is as good a man as he is really when they are together. It leads to this, such a moment, the happiest in years of marriage. In weeks to come they will talk to Nicky, nervously and uselessly, about bad touch. This is good touch, pancakes and the right movie, drink and sex on the floor, a laugh and a kiss, a silly story and a stake through the heart.

CHAPTER 9

PADGETT DOESN'T WANT to be here, but not fiercely. She could go either way. The damp trail goes down, and Kitsune is way ahead of them, whooping with a stick, her half brother hurrying after her half alarmed. The afternoon has brought fog—they drove right into it—and as the sun packs its bags, the mist wets the trees and keeps dripping down. She lets go of Vic's hand for a second, to shake off little drops.

It's been a while. The city, a lot has changed. The Vic, for one thing, has had many stumbles, too numerous, too thorny, too dull to be recounted in their entirety. His move into entertainment was a bad scheme, it turns out. Lawyers and systems guys structured it for themselves, to vanish into the night, and her husband was not sharp enough—or anyway, that's how it got told—to spot it in time. His weakness was blood in the water. He didn't lose it all; he couldn't. In the actual world he hardly fell down one rung. But he's not "the Vic" anymore—younger, coarser men, teeming with sleazy hobbies and boyish, brutal politics, are the ones in the gloss-iest slots. Padgett doesn't miss it. They stay home nights more;

Padgett overheard, six months ago, her husband say at a school function, *We got over ourselves.* It is true. Tough when it happened, but it didn't happen between them. If they were going to divorce, they'd be divorced now. Even the fortune they lost doesn't feel gone, not to Padgett. It was imaginary, more or less.

As for today, it was time. The big local story this morning is a rumor, everywhere onscreen, that one juror in the long-delayed fraud trial of Ariel Park, after ten days of deadlock, threw a chair at another. He hadn't been identified except by race, which leads in the posting to other points, more or less freely associated, about the races of many other participants, and about Ariel Park and the Kitsune School and its power couple founders and some remark from an anonymous source about the propriety of co-opting ancient cultural traditions by the white males dominant in tech, and when Padgett hit this paragraph out loud, Vic stood up from the table and stalked out loudly. The kids were glued to some new episode on the DXM and didn't notice, but Padgett followed him uncertainly back to the master bedroom to find him walking into his walk-in closet. She hadn't been in there herself in who knows how long. He was up on the stepladder, pushing down hats and sandals until he had the cardboard box and stepped back down to her.

"Today, I want to do it," he said to his wife.

Padgett had to think for a minute. The box looked like something summoned onscreen, shelled around some catalog item she'd ordered and forgotten. "OK."

"I'm ready."

"Because of that article? I don't get it. OK, though."

"It's not the article," he said, and handed her the box. He started to strip. He was changing already. "It's just, it's enough."

"Should we tell Kitsune?"

"*No we should not tell Kitsune*," he said, in a disgusted burst, too loudly. "Sorry. But no. They can run around and we can do it."

"Do you want anyone else there?" she asked, but then retreated before he'd snap again, made her own decision and phoned another couple. She took the box back to the kitchen. The kids looked up, Kitsune and then Charles, but she shook her head, the practiced mom gesture of *This is not a present, this is not anything interesting, nothing to see here, nothing for you.*

"Time to get dressed," she said, instead, and dressed now, they walk on down. Vic has the box and she has his arm, almost formally, and they will scatter the ashes of Maureen, his first wife, not in the field where people get married, but in the wide-open space of the amphitheater beyond.

"Don't know if I ever told you this," Vic says, the traditional introduction to a story you've absolutely never heard in your life, or heard dozens of times and always the same way. "But once? Years, years, years ago. I was poking at some issues with our very first launch, at that café on Twenty-Fourth, remember, it's some other place now. Between"—he lets go of her hand to stand with both arms out, weathervaned at right angles so he can place himself in a different neighborhood. The box is along for the ride in his palm—"Castro and Diamond."

"The Meat Market," she says.

"The Meat Market!" he agrees in amazement, back in her arms. "Well suddenly, in the back of the place, there's just a, a tremendous, all this shouting and a chair falls, *ruckus*, and these two guys are just, both of them, locked in, punching and pushing and *whaling* on each other. It was like a bar fight, a bar fight in a movie, and in this quiet place!" Vic is grinning, almost; a bit of manic happiness on the way down to scatter Maureen. "People were like, hey, what the, break it up. And the manager or whoever called the cops obviously, because they came in and pulled them apart. *Spitting* at each other!" They keep walking and, down the road a ways, hear their own yelly children, going at it loud, but any pro parent can tell when it's a fight and when it's, basically, all in fun. "You could just tell," he says, "I mean, whatever, it's ridiculous, but you could just tell it was both their faults. And then, that *night*, these guys from the old *Hyper Magazine* have me over and I sit next to Maureen. That's how we met. Her boyfriend is supposed to be there, and you know what she tells me? That he was at, of course, the Meat Market and, her words, he was *minding his own business* and some guy jumps him and he's arrested and getting stitched up. She can't see him. And I tell her."

"It was both their faults," Padgett says, and smiles. It's like her, growing up with a brother, to interrupt with the punch line. Vic laughs and Padgett laughs too. "And you ended up stealing her from him?"

"I don't know if you'd call it *stealing*," Vic says, as their children yelp around again. "A guy with a broken nose can't take much competition."

"You guys had some fun, right?"

"Not much," Vic says ruefully. "I remember when they shoved me out of the room to work on her, I thought, I was in those green scrubs, *This has got to hurt worse than divorce*."

Padgett doesn't say anything. This is the closest her husband has come to talking about this story canopied over him, of his hated wife, her terrible death. Most hospital scrubs, she thinks, are blue. Aren't they? And from behind them, before anyone can say something, she hears her name, from the only other couple in the park.

Padgett called Rachel and Ben because she knew they'd show. The Nickels are solid friends, their corresponding trails—children at school, departments at work, neighborhoods and concerns—like stones that have become a road to someplace. Marriage too; they haven't split up and regard each other not as mirror images but as some basis for comparison, the way a hat, spotted fallen and trampled on the ground, will make you check your head for yours. They hello all around. "You look good," Ben says, to both of them, a compliment and a faint joke. "What's your secret?"

"I walked out of your wedding," Padgett says, but the laugh is small. They've all figured this out ages ago. In every wedding, it's been cracked, is the makings of another, but that's, like the story they know, not accurate really. Vic wasn't there then. He's just here now.

"No kids?" Padgett asks.

"Soccer," Rachel says ruefully, and then, wind in the trees, a reminder, maybe, that it's a solemn occasion. "You OK?" Rachel asks Vic, a little strangely, she and Vic the farthest points away in their four-cornered drawing. Padgett doesn't say anything. Vic holds up the box. For a minute, from a distance, it likely looks like a box of pastries, that the four of them are picnicking in the gloom, and when the pairs pair up, the men are in no time some fifty, then more, then a hundred yards ahead, out of earshot, in close conference.

Not so many years ago, a photo of these husbands, taken from where the wives are standing, would have led to wild screened speculation. Were they ending the forest? Were they tearing down Bottle Grove? Buying the Masonic temple? Even then it would have been nonsense. You go so far and no farther. You stop getting drunk, you stop sleeping around, or do it less. You get married, or, married, stay married. You make a go. You're less frantic, you make yourself be, about your own sex or money. There might be children distracting you, or you're just, the way houses do in San Francisco neighborhoods built on sand, after any earthquake, settled. You shutter some buildings and walk past them like it's a story in the paper—BODY FOUND IN PARK WAS FRAUDULENT CLERGYMAN, FINGERPRINTS CONFIRM—you don't even click on, not anymore. You get out of the forest but you leave it there. Visit and remember, sometimes, yearn for it even. But civilized people, by definition, don't live in the wild.

What *is* their secret? Both couples talk, all the way down to the amphitheater, coaxed-up secrets, conjured quick, they wouldn't reveal any other day or some other place. "Vic took me down there, this was *years* ago," Padgett is telling Rachel, "to this grouping of warehouses absolutely no place. And in the basement was a *cage*."

"Every so-called mogul," Vic says to Ben, "had to have some weird impossible project, right? Dinner delivered by tiny helicopters, big clock in the desert, green trains, cars driven by ghosts. This complete fraud of a man, Ariel's brother actually, and *fuck* him, sold me the idea. Foxes sense each other, right? They track each other, they trail each other. So we thought we could use animal proteins as the basis for a digital system. So we went here together, *right here*, dead of night, like an old movie, bagged a fox and drove it to a warehouse I owned in deep secret."

"Ben was working late all the time and I started flirting with him in a bar. I mean, I must have been losing my mind." Rachel gestures to the trees around them, as if that were where her mind had gone. "We would walk together, *right here*, me and the vicar. And then he got a place in the Sunset."

"And one day he took her to some rental place," Ben says, and both men look back at their wives. "A faraway neighborhood, right under my nose."

"Do you think something actually happened?" Vic asks.

Ben shakes his head, but maybe not at that. "It wasn't the barman," he says. "I was wrong about that."

"He wasn't torturing the fox in the cage," Padgett says. "I was wrong about that. But—"

"*Nevertheless*," Rachel says, "when he asked for money I gathered as much as I could."

"She pawned *wedding gifts*! About ten thousand in cash, it was." Ben wipes his head, almost completely bald now, his hand shaking with the idea of it.

"It was the first creature on the Trail," Vic says, "but the digital tag killed it. Some beasts are too wild to pin down and cage like that. I was crazy paranoid about what to do. Someone could have found out and that would have been a scandal we couldn't afford. We ended up basically cremating the poor thing just to destroy the little chip we'd put in it to begin with."

"I stole the money back. When she got home she took a shower, and I just grabbed it and went back to faking sleep."

Rachel looks from her husband to the shivery trees. "I think maybe he followed me from the park that night, broke in and stole the money? I don't know."

"—and I never asked him about it again," Padgett says to Rachel.

"—and she never asked me about it," Ben says to Vic.

"—and I never saw him again," Rachel says to Padgett.

"—and we scattered the ashes," Vic says to Ben.

"Already?" Padgett says. They've caught up. Everyone stops talking. With the sunset starting up, the vast space is daunting to everyone but the children, who are screaming wildly at the far end.

"Already what?" Vic asks.

"I thought you said, *scattered the ashes.*"

The two men share a look of completely transparent fake confusion.

"No," Ben says. "Nuh-uh."

"What were you talking about then?" Rachel asks, almost coyly.

"Tech," Vic admits. "You?"

"Children," Padgett admits, pointing out to them. She hasn't told the story, of course, about Martin and their kidnap scheme, not to anyone. Nor has Ben said anything about faking the scandal at school. Rachel never talks about the horse, and Vic hasn't, despite its bubbling underneath every article he reads, said a word to anyone about Ariel Park, soon to be found *not guilty* if he's arranged it right. And he's seemed to. Ariel will disappear in silence, like any failure in a successful town. There are countless secrets around them, and if it seems nothing could be, should be, built on such deceptions, you can think that they leave them here, the place where by decree nothing can be built. They do it now, scatter it away, and they do it quickly, without much ritual, Rachel and Ben standing somewhat solemnly just a few steps from Padgett and her husband. Vic doesn't even know what to say—it seems disloyal to say he misses his wife, what with his wife here beside him— but nevertheless he thinks of Maureen's laughing face, how flushed it would get, over very stupid jokes—and so says simply, "Rest in peace," which who knows if it's true. It rises to the air, falls to the dark and is gone, like a half-finished question.

If this is a story about two marriages—

They troop back out, Kit and Charlie lagging behind now, their arms hanging down, complaining about the uphill climb back. The trees are silhouettes now, dead flat like cut paper. It can be a lonely time of day. Everyone who has to be some-place, home or out, is probably there already. If you have nowhere to go, there's nowhere to be.

Martin Icke, barman, is on the avenue seeing the two couples walk out of the woods. He is not eager to be seen, and anyway he's talking to someone else. "Dude," he says into the phone, and reaches down to ruffle his large, eager dog. "That was *you*?"

"I did *not*," Stanford is saying on the other end, "*throw a chair. I drummed my hands* on the back of the chair, as I *stood up, impatiently*. I swear to you, cap'n, it was not scary."

"Your swearing it already sounds scary," Martin says, and they both laugh a lot. Like the bar, they've survived. It's not thriving, what they have—the jukebox is getting wheezy, and their new flooring has been ravenous for money. Both of them would benefit hugely from some constant—a lover, say, who isn't stark raving batshit—but Martin has figured it's not going to happen. He got himself a dog, the large wet bounding sort that could distract you from a world war, and working for himself with a sledgehammer and six beers, tore down the walls in his apartment so it's open, lighter. He watches old movies when he gets home after closing time, and a piece of dialogue in a beautiful Western—*Mac, you ever been in love? No, I've been a bartender all my life*—was the last of the jigsaw. He has not resigned himself, because he is not resigning. This life, he's on his own, standing watch over a place where people cut loose a little from whatever's collared them, spill out their secrets and go home empty of them. It makes him cry and it makes him laugh, but with Stanford sputtering from the courthouse downtown, he's laughing now.

Padgett sees him. She has been wanting to see him, and there's Martin Icke, laughing into a phone while a big dog, it must be his, stares very adroitly into the trees from which they've emerged. He looks OK. She starts to wave or something, then stops and looks back at everyone else. They haven't noticed. They are looking down the block at the parade.

First it looks religious, with some long, flowing nuns holding papier-maché figures high in the air, but by the time they round the corner Padgett can see—yes—some of them are men, and the figures are, those she can recognize, politicians, some local, and pop music stars, some dead. Next some women in kimonos, if they're women, powdered white and twirling parasols and throwing the pink petals of cherry blossoms like a wrong drawing of snow. Cars honk, and Martin's dog barks, you can hear it, excited and enthused like he's made his fortune. Piñatas, women in sombreros singing a song to them, rows of Chinese children in some uniform banging on glockenspiels either in chaos or according to some blueprint—it just sounds like a bell explosion—Padgett can't fathom. They're in the thick of it now, hula hoops and fiery juggling, clowns tossing candy, people in squared-off suits with buckets full of brochures for real estate and summer camps, propositions that should pass or be repealed, judges who should be recalled or reelected, and an all-tuba marching band, all with thick fake hairy beards and hairy hats in parody, or tribute, to some cultural something she can't identify, or any of it. At this late hour, where can they be going? It will be dark by the time they reach, what else is down there, the zoo? Everyone is delighted and rapt even when the clouds let loose a little and it rains, just a little, on everything. The petals on the concrete lose their pink for violet, like cleaning a palette. Padgett and Martin lock eyes for a little of it, and then he's gone, his big dog too, up to his apartment maybe, if he still lives there, or just tagging along with the cavalcade for the reason of why not, he's a single man in a free country, the parade's for him if he wants it. The children are looking at the raining sky, the adults, both couples here at the exit, at the departing spectacle, feeling ordinary, just human, in comparison. Nobody wants it, all of it, to end.

"So," one of them says, finally. "Shall we go get a drink?"

AUTHOR'S NOTE

Lines from the Adrienne Rich poem "What Kind of Times Are These" appear courtesy of her estate. Lyrics from the Stars song "Turn It Up" appear courtesy of Stars, with particular thanks to Amy Millan and Torquil Campbell.

The author is also grateful to Daisy Fried's poem "Thrash," Harry Mathews's novel *Cigarettes*, Theodore Roethke's book *Straw for the Fire*, Andrew Alan Johnson's study *Ghosts of the New City*, David Weatherly's indescribable *Strange Intruders*, and James Simpson's translation of *Reynard the Fox*. A tip of the hat, too, to the films *Rebecca* and *My Darling Clementine*, and to the pop album from which the novel gets its secret structure.

Thanks more personally to Lisa Brown, Otto Handler, Charlotte Sheedy, Nancy Miller, Lauren Cerand, Suzi Young, Lilliana Elizade, Barbara Darko, and to all the wives and husbands who shared, perhaps foolishly, stories of their marriages, for what is nevertheless, of course, a work of fiction.

A NOTE ON THE AUTHOR

DANIEL HANDLER is the author of the novels *All the Dirty Parts*, *We Are Pirates*, *Why We Broke Up*, *Adverbs*, *Watch Your Mouth*, and *The Basic Eight*. As Lemony Snicket, he is responsible for many books for children, including the thirteen-volume sequence *A Series of Unfortunate Events* and the four-book series *All the Wrong Questions*. He is married to the illustrator Lisa Brown and lives with her and their son in San Francisco.